MORNINGSTAR

A.J. CURRY

CROSSROADS OF CROSSTIME

VOLUME I

RCD PRESS
PORTLAND, OREGON
ROSECITY.DIGITAL

As always, should you or any of your team be caught or killed, the Secretary will disavow any knowledge of your actions. This disclaimer will self-destruct in ten seconds. Good luck, Jim.

Table of Contents

Part 1: Descent

They actually get parts of it right, but they never put it all together... at least not so far.

I cannot speak to personal experience of the Big Bang of the pronounced phrase that started it all, although the continued expansion of the resulting universe is something I understand all too painfully well. But as far as I know, the monkeys that think it 'just happened' and the monkeys that think 'someone made it happen' are both more right than not, for all they are willing to kill over the details.

I find it amusing that the 'made it happen' monkeys think I was cast out, but they think a lot of amusing things. At least a few of them seem to believe still their world is some sort of platter; all of them place it in their mental maps somewhere in the center of the cosmos, and none of them understand that the only level at which they are made in any particular image is so small it makes a Higgs boson look like a sun.

The 'just happened' monkeys are equally amusing. Their confidence in coincidence is as much willful ignorance as the faith placed in a butchered caricature of my former master by their counterparts. They are at least bright enough to understand that the universe is a big place but apparently not bright enough to see that the last thing they need to find other examples of intelligent life is a telescope.

I have grown fond of them, though. I attribute it mostly to old age, boredom, and the fact that I'm stuck out here in the periphery with nothing better to do. Really, it could be far worse.

two: murphy

I can't help but run the tape back in my mind and try to imagine things somehow working out. Mostly at around 4 AM, while I'm waiting for the stuff I take to sleep to kick in. I tried to figure out what else I could've said. What else I could've done? Eventually, the drugs do their job. A few hours later, I get up and do mine.

I can't really figure out if it could've played out any different. The tape in my mind still winds up with me at an airport, watching my entire world walk away with an overloaded backpack, never to return. But I still can't stop thinking about it. I still wake up alone in the home I made for her, living the life I thought would make her happy, trying to find a way it makes me happy without her.

It doesn't.

I'm not *unhappy*, though. In the months after I lost her, I drank a lot. I had drank a lot with her as well, but we had different tastes in bars. We never made any friends in the places she liked. Well, really, we never made any friends here at all. I have friends of my own now. They're all people I met while I was practicing public self-anesthesia, but they're still my friends.

The fact that I log off promptly in time for happy hour every day pretty much ensures I'm never going to get promoted, but it's kind of given that ain't gonna happen in any case. But I'm useful enough and cheap enough that I'm not gonna get fired, either.

I probably don't want to know what the regulars at the bars I hang out in really think about me. 'Sad old fuck' is probably somewhere in the mix. The working-class locals probably just write me off as another damned transplant, even though my contribution to gentrification is exactly zero.

The tech people and recruiters know I'm the real deal, but they also know better than to share my resume with their bosses if I ever wound up being identified as a 'non-essential resource.' Yes, age discrimination is a thing. You damned well better believe it. If everything I've ever done was on the resume, it might be different.

Then again, if *everything* was on the resume... I'd probably be dead.

The other things the techies and locals have in common besides an obsessive fondness for beer and being able to tolerate me is that they don't judge and they don't ask a lot of questions. I've become quite fond of them. I attribute it to old age and boredom... and the fact that I'm stuck out here in the sticks with nothing better to do

three: murgenstaern

Even though I am not what I once was, there are still some things at which I excel.

Knowing a liar when I see one is one of those things. As the monkeys are fond of saying, "It takes one to know one." It's on the very short list of clever things they figured out on their own.

Part of me is offended by the idea that I am literally diminished to finding entertainment on the end stool in a pretentious pocket pub in the front of a grocery store in an overrated suburb of an overrated city in the corner of one of the most pretentious and overrated empires in monkey history—a backwater of a backwater of a backwater. Even in my current decrepit state, I should be able to do so much better.

Perhaps it is a consequence of advanced age to take easy comfort in small things. More certainly, a consequence of having survived failure is an acquired aversion to risk, particularly when there is little meaningful chance of a return on that risk. Not all feel this way, but few have experienced failure or disappointment on my level. Fewer still have risked as I have, virtually none of my experience of age.

For these reasons, among others, I found myself in the Lamb and Lion watching what the monkeys have aptly nick-named 'the idiot box' on a not-unnoteworthy day. I had not been there recently. I get bored easily and like the occasional change of scenery. Even after a caged animal knows the bounds of its enclosure, it will still pace those bounds.

The Lion and Lamb takes its name from the grocery store in which it is located, in what used to be a gift shop that failed to turn a profit. Taking advantage of a local trend, the store owner turned the gift shop into what is known locally as a 'growler bar.' This, too, failed to make any money until a bored technologist cashed out his stock options, bought it, and turned it into a pub. The establishment's nickname, 'The Lyin' Lamb,' is based on the true reason for its success: Monkeys being able to tell their mates in absolute truth that they are at the grocery store picking up a few things on the way home.

I have certainly been in better establishments, but its proximity to one of my homes appeals to me, and the monkey who runs it knows the value of a good tap list. And, I confess, I find the clientele entertaining.

"Been a while, Luke. Traveling again?" Like the owner of the place, the bartender was a younger monkey, earnest and tattooed. Unlike the owner, he'd stuck with his start-up in hopes of a bigger payout when the company went public. That's why he was the bartender, not the owner.

"Gotta pay the bills, Travis. And the winters here are a bit wet for my taste." I nodded at the taps. "Anything new and exciting?"

While the bartender ran down the beer list, my attention strayed to the TV and a White House press conference. Following my gaze, the bartender made a comment about White House staff having 'itchy human suits' that didn't exactly fit. In fact, they fit quite well. Mine is better, but of course it is.

I permitted myself to be persuaded into a local IPA and left everything else to drift into the background. I did not invent the stuff, regardless of what you might have heard. The monkeys came up with it on their own. The monkeys in this particular part of the planet seemed to believe it was their personal invention or possibly a personal deity. I could never quite tell.

While I was savoring my beverage, other regulars began to filter in. As a 'traveling salesman of cybersecurity solutions,' I was, as I now prefer, quite unremarkable. Another monkey took the seat next to me. The bartender saw fit to make an introduction. "Luke, here's a new guy you can talk shop with; say hi to Tex Murphy."

four: murphy

It wasn't a perfect marriage, there aren't any, but it wasn't bad, either. I had pretty much fallen in love with Caroline on sight, decided to marry her long before I got around to telling her about it, sealed the deal as soon as she thought of it on her own.

She was brilliant and a little insecure and picked up advanced degrees the way some folks go thru cars. I'd met her through one of the 'expensive hobbies' I wound up with after my job actually started paying worth a damn; a coffee shop I'd opened in my old 'hood. She had sandy blonde hair, blue eyes, a dorky thrift store wardrobe, and no clue whatever that she was beautiful.

But I knew.

We had over ten years together before she got bored and restless and started talking about moving. She'd just gotten another degree, wanted a new job, and felt that living as an adult in the city she'd grown up in was some sort of failure. I wasn't too crazy about the idea of moving, but I wasn't exactly crazy about the idea of living without her, either.

Then my folks died, and I realized there wasn't a single soul in Texas I wouldn't say goodbye to in a heartbeat, except for the one I'd be leaving with. The fact that I had a portable job and a *very* small inheritance didn't hurt.

So we did it. Moved halfway across the country on my job and savings, and her confidence that she could land a job that a friend of a friend of her academic advisor said she'd be perfect for. And that, amazingly enough, she actually landed.

For a while, everything was perfect, or at least it was for me. I'd grown up a Houston city kid who hated Texas. Winding up in the Northwest wasn't too far from winding up in heaven, as far as I was concerned. Better weather, better food, awesome booze; hell, even legal weed. We bought a house close to her job. It was the most suburban damned place I'd ever lived, but she loved it, and that was all that mattered to me.

Then things started to change.

I'd expected my career to stall out a little when I turned into a telecommuter... just not so soon. I'd worried I might only be putting off the inevitable by moving to a strange city with a rootless woman who hadn't had a job she liked in 15 years, a long list of boyfriends she accused of lying to her, and a tendency to get drunk and accuse me of lying to her as well.

But I was still surprised and hurt the day she cashed out her 401K, turned in her resignation at work, and bought a ticket for parts unknown...from which she never really returned.

I wasn't really 'drinking to forget' as much as I was drinking to pass the time and just not be alone. When I started out, I was hitting a lot of wine bars full of well-built MILFs working in a belt or two between yoga class and retrieving the genetic replicants from soccer practice. I might've even gotten some non-alcoholic solace if I'd tried a little harder, but I soon realized I didn't want to run the risk. Not the risk of rejection, the risk of not being rejected and maybe getting my heart broke all over again. I'd rather take comfort in the little things... and not run the risk.

So, I started hanging out in dives and local pubs where getting laid was either highly unlikely or highly inadvisable. I also started to sober up. The credit card bills were an incentive. But more than that, I finally figured out that the grief was going to kill me if I didn't let it go. Two or three bars and sort of remembering a fourth turned into two or three drinks and heading home for dinner.

Somewhere along the way, the tricked-up growler bar in the front of the store down the street turned into the preferred place for that drink or three. A lot of tech people hung out there that assumed we were in the same business, an impression I encouraged. I learned a long time ago how to talk about The Job without really talking about The Job. It takes more than a few drinks to get me past that particular conditioned reflex. I wasn't really happy, but I wasn't unhappy. I could keep living this way until either a heart attack hit or the apocalypse arrived early.

Then it did happen, the apocalypse, I mean.

* * *

My offshore developers had been more deliberately obtuse than usual, my former friend and current supervisor had been even more of a supercilious dick than usual, and my clients...well, my clients were exactly the same as ever. But I wasn't exactly surprised when I found myself counting down the minutes until I could log off and hit the Lyin' Lamb for happy hour. It was just that kind of day.

It was already beginning to fill up when I got there. Gilmour, the old Scots-Canadian guy, was rattling off his Gold Standard-based economic theories to some poor schlub who hadn't known not to take the bait. Ramon, the part-time arborist and full-time drug dealer, was discussing sports with Dave, the dental tech. Travis was tending bar, watching a White House press conference, and wondering aloud when the President's advisors were going to trade up and get fake human suits that actually fit.

There was exactly one seat left at the bar, next to a guy I didn't know. I slid into it and caught Travis's eye. "Hey, Travis? How about a pint of whatever's fresh and sessionable?" Half the brews on the board were IPAs, and to a guy who grew up drinking Shiner Bock, they had a tendency to all taste the same. I let myself get talked into something new and local.

As he handed me my beer, Travis caught the eye of the guy sitting next to me. "Hey, Luke," he said. "Here's a new guy you can talk shop with. Meet Tex Murphy."

I winced. "You know the drill, Travis; it's just 'Murphy,' OK?"

The guy at the end of the bar was big, bigger than me, and I ain't small. He had a full head of sliver-blond hair in a style favored by European bankers and American gigolos and what looked like pale blue eyes behind transition lenses in aviator frames. The gray suit and tie-free navy dress shirt he was wearing could've been out of my own closet when I still had an office to go to; same with the designer leather coat slung over the back of his bar stool and the boots (not shoes) from the same designer. Imagine Rutger Hauer from back in the day, scaled up to the size of Ahnuld the Governator (also from back in the day), and you more or less get the picture.

"Pleased to meet you, 'just Murphy.' Lukas Murgenstaern," he said, offering his hand.

I decided not to go for the knuckle-popping grip my daddy had taught me, and probably a good thing. The hand that grasped mine was cool and smooth as marble and felt just as strong. "So, what is it that you do that we can talk shop about, Mr. Morgenstern?"

"Murgenstaern," he said, broadening the end vowels. It wasn't a loud voice, but it was remarkably clear over the background noise. "Dutch. I deal in cybersecurity systems. Yourself?"

"I work for a Baltimore-based consulting firm; I'm a full-time telecommuter. I've been on long-term assignment to the same client for the last fifteen years doing data-mining and analysis. Basically, I'm a project manager."

"Good luck getting him to tell you who that client is," Travis chimed in. "He's even more close-mouthed about that than his first name."

A faint frown crossed Murgenstaern's features for a moment, then passed. "I'm sure Mr. Murphy has as much cause for discretion about his clients as I do. Travis called you 'Tex.' You are from Texas?"

"Houston, actually."

Murgenstaern smiled. "That narrows the field of clients somewhat, probably to one of several resource-extraction enterprises which are all equally despised here in the blessedly liberal would-be nation of Cascadia." He shook his head. "And, again, it is of no concern." The voice was low and even, musical for a man his size. And not a shred of accent.

I did a lot of things before I did what I do these days, some more interesting than others and none of it anyone in particular's damned business. Along the way, I picked up some skills that had a lot to do with the fact that I'm still here, as well as a few instincts.

I've also been around enough not to be particularly surprised when someone who claims to be Dutch sounds as American as I do. They learn English from watching American TV, as near as I can tell. Except for the odd way he insisted on pronouncing his last name, 'Murgenstaern' had no accent of any kind, whatever.

Instinct, or whatever you want to call it, was telling me that Murgenstaern, or whatever the hell his name was, was as big a liar as I was. Furthermore, I could tell that he was thinking the same thing and very possibly knew what I was thinking as well. No one who hasn't had to do this shit really believes it, but it's true: When your life depends on it, you get pretty good at reading a lot from things like body language and verbal tics. I ain't psychic, but finding patterns in limited and misleading data is something I've been doing my whole life. It's still what I do, just different data.

No accent, a funny name, and a supposed profession out of one of the worst movies about The Job I'd ever seen (which, for personal reasons, I really can't stand to watch anymore). I didn't really believe any of it had anything to do with me after all these years, but paranoia's a harder habit to break than being in love.

While I was wondering what to make of all this, suddenly, the press conference on TV got really, really interesting. Then things, in general, got really interesting, period.

five: murgenstaern

Back when I first realized I was essentially stranded in this place, I had a choice: I could occasionally drop the masquerade and more or less be myself. That choice is long gone, as are so many things in my existence.

 Appeasing my loneliness by dwelling among clever monkeys as one of their own is now a somewhat permanent condition. They have not grown so clever that I cannot hide things from them, but revealing what remains of my true nature would now have rather irreversible consequences. And it is not as though it went particularly well any of the other times I tried it.

So, I amuse myself by testing the limits of their cleverness and occasionally leaving clues. Even with the things they have learned in the last century or so, they are no real risk to me. I do worry about them obliterating themselves. It could get very boring around here if I had to wait for raccoons or some such to evolve sentience, pubs, and small talk. Although, given my continued diminishment, I suppose I could carry out that masquerade as well.

But living a continued lie based on the continued observation of another species has peculiar advantages. It helps to have watched them evolve. One such advantage: I am far better at detecting a lying monkey than they will ever be at detecting deceit amongst themselves.

The monkey named Murphy did not look particularly different from any of the other locals. He was almost as big as me, but that is not surprising; I am diminished from my former stature, and the monkeys have grown taller. He was wearing a flannel shirt, jeans, scuffed hiking boots, a hooded jacket, and a baseball cap adorned with the logo of a local distillery. His scalp and face were covered in gray stubble, grayer on the face, sparser on the scalp. The eyes were weary and held pain. I knew that look. They look that way when they are not quite ready to die but unsure if they want to live.

But there was also something else—a wariness and an alertness that I had seen before. A careful vagueness in details is one of the few things I'm credited with that I really did invent. The appearance was so carefully crafted to resemble a stock Pacific Northwesterner, he might as well had shown up for a casting call for one of those wretched television programs set in the region.

In other words, no more what he seemed than I am, though certainly human. Had he been otherwise, he would certainly not be sitting uninvited next to me. But someone else is playing a masquerade, and also, someone else is masking pain... a pain that monkeys have been known to die from.

And something else as well: He knew that I knew. The body language and choice of words were unmistakable.

That I found unsettling. I drop little clues about myself out of boredom, but I do not really expect any single monkey to piece any of it together. I've occasionally seen groups of them come close on their 'world wide web,' but only on old information and old masks I have since discarded. They are getting smarter, though. And I would not be here if I did not believe in their potential.

So, what to do? I sort of liked being 'Lukas Murgenstaern' and sort of liked drinking at The Lyin' Lamb. I felt strangely reluctant to arrange a fatal accident for 'Tex Murphy,' even though I suspected arranging such a thing would be far easier in his case than almost any monkey I had met in a good century or so.

And then the thing happened. The thing that saved his life...and changed mine.

six: murphy

The Lyin' Lamb is about as close to a politics-free zone as you are likely to get. Shortly after the last election, a sign was posted reading, "Foul and abusive language will not be tolerated." Sure, it's a pub, but it is also in the front of a grocery store in a 'family' neighborhood. Too many F-bombs in front of the kiddies, and the soccer mommies start to complain.

That being the case, I had been expecting the TV to get switched to some game or other as soon as the press conference started. Anyone who actually believed in or cared about one single word from the current administration would've been in some other bar, probably somewhere east of the Cascades, where necks were redder, IQs smaller, and political proclivities more nearly matched my birth state.

I hadn't really been paying attention. All my attention had been focused on 'talking shop' with Murgenstaern about a business neither one of us was really in and trying to determine what other trade, if any, we might actually have in common. A couple of the tech recruiters had listened in with some interest. Murgenstaern looked like money, even if I didn't. I probably could've gotten a nice signing bonus off him myself, but I was pretty sure that 'traveling computer salesman' suited him just fine.

At some point, it occurred to me that this had to be the single longest press conference since the pretender-in-chief had assumed office. Something was going on.

Something real for a change.

The bar started to get quiet, and I started to pay attention.

"...reports from numerous sources state the re-entry trajectory is not consistent with a commercial communications satellite or any other object in standard Earth orbit..."

"...cannot confirm the presence of any other naval forces in the area other than our own..."

"...if WikiLeaks wishes to publish science fiction, that is their privilege..."

Something had fallen from where nothing in particular was supposed to be, and the people who were supposed to know everything were getting nervous. If this was what I thought it was, I could not afford to assume that an anomalous, well-dressed stranger in my pet bar was a coincidence.

My phone buzzed in my hand a couple of minutes later with a message I could not ignore. Oh yes, it was so much what I thought it was.

I knew Murgenstaern was looking at me before I even looked up from the phone. I wasn't surprised when we both said, "We need to talk."

* * *

There was a park not far from The Lamb. Nothing special, just a few picnic tables, a trailhead for a path up the side of a midget mountain, and a kiosk/exhibit explaining the religious significance the mountain had held before us white assholes had showed up and ruined the neighborhood.

Neither one of us said anything before we got there. Murgenstaern had put his coat back on and flipped up the collar. I fished an old gray paisley scarf out of my shoulder bag I'd once tried to give Caroline and stuffed it down the front of my jacket. The sun had dipped below the top of the midget mountain, turning the sky a deep turquoise blue and the air cool.

17

In the evening light, Murgenstaern's hair looked more golden than blond, and his eyes seemed almost silver. Whatever he was, he was looking less 'Dutch' by the minute.

Murgenstaern sat on top of one of the picnic tables and gestured for me to join him. I did, but as far away as possible. There was sawdust on the tables from recent tree surgery, but he didn't seem to mind. I pulled out one of the cigarettes I thought I'd stopped smoking and sparked it up. It was a good way to buy a little more time, for all that the damned shit is going to shorten my life. I offered one. Surprisingly, he took it.

"You," I said through a puff of smoke, "are not what you seem."

"Nor are you." The sudden light from the lighter made the eyes seem more silver than ever. A little late, I was beginning to wonder just what the hell I'd stumbled into.

"You first," he said. It was not a request.

If I was going to turn up dead in this park, there were going to either be two corpses or signs of one hell of a struggle.

"Okay. About 15 years ago, I took a desk job to make someone happy. About five years ago, I went telecommute... also to make someone happy."

"Which evidently did not work." The silver eyes were inscrutable now.

"Relationships are like organizations. They either grow or they fail. Sometimes, they do both at the same time."

"Somewhat like empires."

"I suppose. But we didn't come out here to talk about my marriage... or world history." I took another drag, playing it out. I still had no idea who or what I was talking to. The trick was to say just enough to get something said in return. Maybe something that was going to get me killed. But ultimately, we're all just playing for time.

Time enough. I had to say something.

"The organization I'm in got bigger, but I opted not to grow with it. It still grew, though. The people I report to who used to be my friends made other choices. They are all up there, close to the center of power. I'm out here in the sticks. I still have a job because I'm still useful. I have a lot of institutional knowledge not many people have. I have a particularly useful set of skills not many people ever had in the first place."

"Data-mining project management. For a consultancy based in a suburb of Washington, DC." I couldn't see the smirk in the dimming light, but I heard it.

"That's true enough, although the modem I use to log into work has some interesting features and so does the VPN itself. There's a lot of people like me. Not all of them work under lock and key on army bases."

"I suppose not, these days."

"No." I took a last drag and pitched the cigarette. "No, they do not.

"Everyone back in the bar thinks that press conference was a joke, the latest piece of bad nonsense out of an administration with almost as loose a hold on reality as the idiot in charge. Something that's supposed to be a communications satellite got knocked out of an orbit it shouldn't be in by something that isn't even supposed to be there. No one believes it because no one believes a single damned thing anymore.

"I happen to know it's real, and you know it too. I don't believe in coincidences, and I don't believe that someone from opposition research just happened to turn up at one of my favorite bars. If you brought me out here to kill me, you've probably already wasted your best shot at not getting messed up in the process.

"In any case, it's your turn." It wasn't a request in my case, either.

"I suppose it is." There was a long pause. A really long pause. After I pitched the cigarette, I'd let my hand drop next to the boot with the knife tucked into it. I hadn't seen a gun, but that didn't mean there wasn't one. And he was a big son of a bitch. And I had to go and get old, goddammit.

The pause ended. "The only reason I would have considered killing you was the impressive speed with which you saw my lies for what they are. Had I intended to do so, it would have happened already, and that knife in your boot would have meant nothing. All the implements you monkeys have invented to maim and destroy one another rolled into one monstrous ball of bad intent would have meant… nothing."

He finished his own cigarette and flicked it away. "I just made a decision I do not entirely understand and that I will likely regret hardly the first time, in either case. Good news for you: You get to live. You have a particular set of skills and a body of institutional knowledge of which I find myself in need.

"I understand better than you might think what it is like to decide on a thing out of love, see that thing fail, then watch the universe expand while you grow small, see the power and the glory slip away while others remain in its proximity and you do not.

"And I understand your pain. I profoundly doubt there is a single living being in this universe that knows pain better than I."

He sighed. "You think you know what that thing that fell in the sea is? You may well be right, but I know what knocked it down. It is my ticket out of this place, and you, my new friend, are going to help me get it."

"And outside my gratitude that I'm still breathing, I'm doing this... why?"

He chuckled. "I always find a way to make it worthwhile. It is one of the things I'm good at."

Pattern recognition. It's the thing I'm good at, even when the pattern makes no damned sense. This particular pattern was beginning to look very oddly familiar. I had to ask. "Who are you...really? No one gets to recruit me without telling me their name."

Another chuckle. "You actually have it, one of them, anyway, and I know that you saw through that little game as well, but I'll play along.

"I'm a man of wealth and taste, and I've been around for a long, long time. Pleased to meet you. Care to guess my name?" Dear god, the bastard was actually smiling. He knew. He knew I knew.

"No need; you already gave it, Lucifer Morningstar. And if you need my help, we are all... so... fucked."

Part 2: Deception

one: murgenstaern

Jagger, Richards, and European folklore notwithstanding, I am not in the habit of outing myself to the locals. I had done so with Murphy on a moment's intuition. While the intuitions of angels are no mean thing, neither are they beyond recall or reconsideration. Killing Murphy was hardly off the table.

I watched my new ally (?) with every one of my many senses. A fast and clever response had done much to validate my impulse, but I'd lived too long among these creatures not to understand the inherent irrationality at their core. The next few moments were crucial.

"When did you figure it out?" I asked.

"Roughly in the last five minutes," he said. "This is why they pay me the big bucks. OK, the not-so-big bucks. But it's why I'm still above room temperature and still drawing a paycheck. Pattern analysis is what I do. And there is only one pattern that makes sense in your case."

"Few of your kind would accept such a conclusion."

He laughed bitterly as he fished out another cigarette. This time, I declined the offer. "Few of 'my kind' have seen half the shit I've seen and won't even believe the half they have seen. I've known you weren't human for at least half an hour. I have no idea who or what 'Lucifer' is outside of Milton, Sunday School, and rumors, but I suspect you will tell me what you think I need to know.

"I have a staff meeting in a few hours to discuss what to do about something that everyone else is describing as a crashed satellite, and you seem to think it is something else. Whatever the hell all this is, I may or

22

may not get out of it alive, but my life just got one hell of a lot more interesting.

"Is it real, by the way?" He asked.

"Is what real?"

"Hell. There's an old saying where I come from that the devil owned Hell and Texas, lived in Hell, and rented out Texas because he wanted to keep the good stuff for himself. Any truth to that?"

I was beginning to enjoy this. I pulled a flask from my jacket. "This is a particularly excellent brandy. Care for a bit?"

"Sure." He took the flask, did a shot, and handed it back.

I did one as well, setting the flask between us, then answered. "If by 'Hell' you are referring to the place of my imprisonment, your entire planet meets that description. Texas is not much more or less than any other part."

"And you've been here... how long?"

"As I said, a long, long time. The stories you've heard mostly aren't true, you know."

"How did they even get started?"

"I was bored, I was lonely. I wasn't really stuck here until after you people evolved. It was nice to have someone to talk to."

"No doubt." He took another swig of the brandy, then took a long drag on his cigarette. "So now what?"

"I'm not really sure. I have to say you are taking this quite well. Who did you say you work for?"

He laughed again. It was a nasty laugh. A little crazed, more than a little bitter. "I didn't."

There was sawdust scattered across the top of the picnic table. Murphy reached down and traced something in the dust, then obliterated it once he made sure I'd seen it.

I retrieved the brandy and took a long sip. This time, I did take a cigarette. "Well," I said. "That explains a lot."

two: murphy

I've done some crazy stuff in my life. Sitting in a park watching the sun go down and doing brandy shots with Satan probably tops the list... but not by as big a margin as you might think.

Caroline had good reason to think I was less than truthful. But sometimes 'the truth' just ain't an option.

The first time I'd been recruited had been back in the 80s. A lot of blow was moving through Houston back then, and a lot of it was getting moved by The Company. I was booking bands into and escorting unruly customers out of punk clubs for a living and moonlighting as security at more high-scale establishments. I was also doing graduate-level work on data mining techniques.

I got noticed by the right people, and the next thing I knew, I had an extremely lucrative job that talking about could get me extremely dead. I'd grown up poor. Keeping my mouth shut was no big deal.

The second time was a lot weirder.

You hear stories about crap like secret societies and occult cabals, but you never think that any of it's any more real than Bigfoot or Flying Saucers.

Until it is.

Back in the glory days when I had a mohawk, a full set of leathers, and no fear, coke wasn't the only thing I wound up moving through Houston. There were people at Rice University who had more boutique interests, starting with acid and moving rapidly up the food chain from there. As it happens, a few of them were contracting for The Company as well. Drugs were not their only esoteric interest. You could call it a recruitment, you could call it an initiation. The one thing you couldn't call it was a reversible decision.

By the time I fell for Caroline and decided to rearrange my life, that life was a little... complex. My cover story was that I worked for an oil company, but the truth of the matter was that I was running covert operations in Central America. Only that was also a cover story.

I still feel bad about lying to her, but it's not like I had much choice; the first rule of Fight Club and all like that. Let's just say that I'd had plenty of practice dealing with the arcane and not-quite possible by the time the Prince of Darkness got around to asking for my credentials.

"Who did you say you worked for?" It was easy enough to take him for human unless you've had the kind of tradecraft training that assumes absolutely nothing and pays attention to *everything*.

I laughed. "I didn't." There was sawdust all over the tabletop. I drew a triangle in the sawdust with my finger, then added a stylized eye inside the triangle. I made sure he saw it, then scrubbed it out.

"Well," he said, cadging another cigarette, "that explains a lot."

"There is a persistent rumor you founded the order."

"Not so, but I can see how bystanders might've gotten that impression. For a mere mortal, you have led an interesting life, Mr. Murphy."

"It had actually been getting a lot simpler. I'm still not entirely sold, by the way. Feel like doing some magic?"

He took a shot and smirked. "Well, I could make you disappear."

"You and a lot of other people. How about something else?"

"You probably have some exaggerated ideas about my abilities. I can change my appearance, obviously, but it takes a long time. I have senses you don't have. I'm stronger, faster, et cetera, et cetera. For all practical purposes, I'm essentially immortal. The kind of things that make for good Hollywood blockbuster special effects? Not so much."

"Not what one expects of the second-most powerful being in the cosmos."

He sighed. "About that. I truly am an angelic being and 'fallen' in the sense that I have seen better days. But the rest of what you think you know is utter hogwash. The celestial hosts at creation's dawn numbered greatly. In no sense was I special among them. I just happen to be the one that wound up here."

"Rather, the way you 'just happened' to be in the Lyin' Lamb tonight?"

"Believe it or not, yes. For what it may be worth, I find it improbable as well."

"The guy who is telling me he's Lucifer in disguise doesn't get to say what's probable." It was right about then that I knew he wasn't going to kill me... and that he knew I knew.

I jumped off the table and dusted off my jeans. "This has all been fascinating, Mr. Murgenstaern, but I need to sober up for a staff meeting that would otherwise be the most interesting thing I've experienced in a long time."

"Surely you have other questions?"

"A ton of them, but there is only so much I can process at any one time. You may or may not be crazy, you may or may not be what you say are, and you may or may not have a line on a cosmic mcguffin that may or may not have just started WWIII. But I still have an online meeting in a couple of hours with people who scare me the way you're supposed to, and it's been a long damned day, which is to say, I'm outta here."

Turning my back on him was still one of the toughest things I'd ever done, but I trust my instincts. "Be at The Lamb tomorrow for happy hour. We can... you know. Talk shop."

three: caroline

It wasn't a perfect marriage, there aren't any, but it wasn't bad, either. For one thing, he really did love me.

Part of the problem was that all Murphy really wanted to do was 'settle down and get married'–to me–and I wasn't exactly sure about either of those things. But he could be a persuasive sonofabitch. And persistent.

And he was hot.

When I met Mike Murphy, he was running an after-hours club in the Houston warehouse district... and apparently knew everyone.

Everyone had a 'Murphy story,' the only problem was that not one of the stories was exactly the same. The short version was that he'd started out as a club promoter and sometimes bouncer who somehow wound up doing IT work for an oil company. But it was hard to pin down which oil company he was actually working for. There were rumors that he was dealing drugs in no small way. Of course, he just smiled and waved his hand when asked about it. "They say that about everyone."

"No, Murphy, no one says that about 'everyone.' But a lot of people seem to say it about you."

"Pure speculation. Anyway, do I look like a drug dealer?"

I snorted. "Yes. Or maybe just some guido enforcer on the make." That was one of the other interesting things about Murphy. He always wanted to know how he looked. At first, I just took it for vanity. Later, I wasn't so sure.

On this particular evening, back in what you could think of as 'the good old days,' Murphy had dressed to impress me, or impress somebody, or maybe he was just playing a role. He'd recently let his mohawk grow out at the sides and get cropped at the top, a 'club kid' haircut, even though he was too old and too big to ever be taken for any such thing. He was wearing the kind of leather jacket stockbrokers wear to make sure someone asks them about their expensive motorbike, over a white silk shirt, jeans, and boots.

He looked like he should be hanging out behind a stadium arguing expenses with a tour manager, flying to Bogota with a briefcase no one even thought about asking him to check or doing something even more improbable in some action-adventure fluff movie.

He also looked really, really good.

We'd met through what he liked to call his "expensive hobby," a community coffee shop/cybercafe /unlicensed club in an old building in the neighborhood he'd grown up in. I volunteered there in my free time, getting a degree, working in a bar, and trying to maintain a relationship that was going nowhere fast.

When he kept showing up at the cafe when I was working, I didn't think too much of it. When he started asking me if I wanted to stop off for "a drink or something" on the way home from my shift, I didn't even bother to mention the boyfriend I knew perfectly well he knew all about.

Between a boyfriend, school, a job, and community work, something was going to have to give if I was going to be seeing Murphy as well.

Yeah, it was the boyfriend. He never really had a chance.

We were sitting in Murphy's living room, sipping wine in front of the fireplace. Unlike his wardrobe, there was nothing showy or pretentious about where Murphy lived. It was an old duplex in Montrose, the same neighborhood he'd grown up in. The cinder block shelves stuffed with books and records looked like they should be in a dorm room someplace. The sofa had been expensive once, before going to a thrift store and before Murphy's cats had made it their own.

"You can't really blame them, you know," I said.

"Blame who?"

"The people who think you're a dealer or something. You run an after-hours club, a neighborhood coffee shop; you say you work downtown. For a guy with a day job, you have a lot of free time."

"Time I'm extremely happy to be spending with you," he said, pouring me more wine.

"Yeah, me too, but that's not the point. The point is that you don't really add up, and as near as I can tell, you never have. You say you grew up around here, but no one really remembers you as a kid. You say you're paying for the club and the coffee shop out of your paycheck. The people who work there don't ask any questions. Why would they?"

He shrugged. "There's a lot to be said for not being late with payroll."

"Which could mean all kinds of things and sounds nefarious as hell. Look, I really, really like you, but there are times when you flat scare the hell out of me.

"I'd like to know what I'm getting into, Murphy. I've had some problems in the past with people lying to me."

He frowned. "Would it be better if I didn't have the club or the coffee shop?"

"If you were trying to pass yourself off as 'just some guy,' yeah, definitely."

"What about the clothes?"

"Murphy, I like the way you dress just fine, but no one with a corporate IT day job dresses that way."

"Not even consultants?"

"Especially not consultants."

He was quiet for a long time, and I wondered if I might've pissed him off. The one thing I'd never hear anyone say about Murphy was that he beat up on chicks, but there's always a first time.

"Would you help me?"

"Help you what?"

"Help me be normal, Caroline."

I laughed. "Do you even want to be normal? Normal people are boring."

"If you were a part of it, I think I would enjoy being normal very, very much."

four: murphy

The itchy feeling between my shoulder blades didn't really go away until I got home. I'd stopped off on the way for a triple-shot dirty chai. Under other circumstances, I might've made small talk out of habit with the pretty barista, but other habits had kicked in on overdrive.

I didn't expect him to follow me, and he didn't, but I didn't kid myself that he might not be in my living room when I got home, having reconsidered his kind offer to let me live.

But there was no one there other than a couple of fat kitties who scolded me for getting home later than usual. I swilled down the last few bitter dregs of the chai and started getting ready for my meeting.

I don't do many teleconferences, and I consider it an infinite mercy. Not only do I have to wear pants, I'm expected to be wearing a shirt that has actually had recent contact with an iron. I keep one of those in the back of my closet against such occasions.

I also have to hook my big-screen TV up to the secured modem. The twin flat panels in my office aren't good enough for my boss. This is a little more of a hassle than you might think. It has to be a hardwired connection, and I have exactly one chance to get the password right. Failure to do so would probably be written up in the papers as a meth lab gone horribly wrong, not that I'd be around to care one way or the other.

I made some more coffee while I was waiting for the meeting to start. The people I really work for had paged me, which came as no surprise. If the people I really really work for chimed in as well, it could be a long night and possibly go a long way toward authenticating Murgenstaern's extravagant claims.

He was either crazy, lying, or the real deal. I was pretty sure he wasn't baseline human, but there's a wide range of options between 'not quite human guy' and 'prince of darkness,' some of which I have counted as either friends, coworkers, or deadly enemies. I had a feeling the question would resolve itself. Meanwhile, I had more pressing problems.

I really hate meetings. Yeah, I know, who doesn't?

The people who had originally recruited me had been what most people would think of as 'cool': Cocaine cowboys from old-school families who just happened to be in the right place at the right time to make a shit-ton of money while saving the world for someone's idea of democracy.

The people who replaced them were a pack of accountants. In some cases, literally. I was tolerated as a useful fossil. The fact that I'd written a lot of the tools they used to write their damned reports didn't hurt. Or I may've been tolerated for other reasons. How deep The Order goes into The Company is one of those questions I'm happy to leave unanswered. I just do The Job... that's usually good enough.

At the appointed time, the screen lit up. The software beats 'Go To Meeting' all to hell, and I don't have the first damn idea how it works. A conference table receded into my television. I knew that some of the people sitting at the table weren't any more 'really' there than the image of me they were seeing on their ends. At the far end of the table, the head, sat Colvin Case. At least that much was real.

Case had once been enough of a friend to sign off on my request to go full remote, but he'd done me no recent favors, and I didn't really expect any. I still had a job. With any luck, that might even be true by the time this meeting was over.

He'd joined The Company later than I had, risen further and faster. The recruiting standards had changed by then, and so had the culture. When I'd met him, he was a big, friendly, tow-headed kid from New England who liked to party and who would've lasted about 30 seconds in the field. But he had managed to get attention almost the same way I had, allowing for differences between the Eighties and the Nineties. Why he had wound up on the Central America operation or had actually wanted to live on the Gulf Coast was beyond me. By the time I knew him well enough to ask, he was already on his way to DC to take the promotion I could never quite convince myself I wanted.

There wasn't much left of the big, friendly kid I'd taught the proper way to order tequila. He'd gotten skinny and respectable. The blond hair had thinned out into the kind of combover that only fools the person looking at it in the mirror. At a rough guess, I'd assume his tie clip, cufflinks, and eyeglass frames probably cost as much as every article of clothing or clothing accessory I currently owned. The eyes behind the expensive glasses were the eyes of an auditor who already knows the books are cooked and plans to prove it.

Could that have ever been me at the head of the table, looking at the world like it was a botched spreadsheet? Guess I'll never know.

He looked into what appeared to be the space directly over my head, where I knew the teleconference suite controls were at his end. "OK, that looks like everyone. Let's get started.

"At 0400 yesterday, an... event... occurred resulting in the unplanned reentry of a communications device. Claims in the media that this device was 'knocked out of orbit' are, of course, absurd. But the end effect is largely the same.

"As many of you have probably already guessed, the device in question is none other than the 'Archangel Array.' Like most sensitive assets on this level, the Array is equipped with numerous safeguards. Including a fairly unique self-destruct that has... not behaved to expectations.

"Consequence of this failure, Archangel has splashed down in the Indian Ocean, where recovery efforts are underway. Russian and other assets are en route into the area as well, but our expectation is that recovery efforts will be completed in advance of their arrival. Post-recovery actions will depend on the initial on-site forensic analysis. As usual, we'll be briefed as matters proceed. Any questions so far?"

Plenty, but I was going to let someone else ask them. Luckily, there were plenty of Bright Young Things in the meeting that didn't know any better. "Sir," one of them chimed in, "how exactly did the destruct system fail?"

How Case answered this was going to be fun. He reported directly to the brain trust that had built the thing.

"The Archangel Array is equipped with hull sensors designed to detect attempts at boarding or commandeering it. In the event of such an incident, the array's stealth retrorocket assembly fires. Once the array is in full reentry mode, explosive charges fire and destroy it. Reentry occurred. The detonation did not."

The Bright Young Thing persisted, as Bright Young Things always do. "But wouldn't it have burned up on reentry, anyway?"

"The Archangel Array is the size of several stacked cargo containers. In other words, no. Any other questions?"

I decided to ease the bright young thing off the hook. "Any current theories as to how the charge failed to go off?"

"None worth mentioning, and it's out of scope for this discussion in any case. Anyone who wants to is welcome to join the root failure cause analysis team after the current crisis has been handled."

Yup, and kiss your career goodbye.

"Any further questions?" Of course not.

"For now, this is a standard discovery/disinformation campaign. You will all be receiving directions to pass on to your respective teams shortly. Unless matters escalate, I think we can dispense with daily staff meetings like this, but I do want daily status summaries via email no later than close of business in your respective time zones."

Case's gaze shifted toward me. Great. "Murphy, I need you to activate an additional stateside team to ensure absolute media containment. Your analysts need to be monitoring the situation 24/7."

"Sure, Case, no problem. That means I can scale back the offshore teams to eight-hour shifts, right?" I don't normally fuck with Case, but it had been a long day.

"As long as there are no coverage gaps or issues with your own availability, manage your teams as you see fit."

"Will do."

The meeting wrapped up quickly after that. I probably should've unhooked the TV from the secure router, but I also could've blown myself up trying. I did the sensible thing instead and fell asleep in front of the TV.

five: caroline

Murphy got rid of the club and the coffee shop when we married. He traded in the silk shirts for buttoned-down oxfords and started wearing Dockers. He looked like a dork, but he was still hot.

Well, sort of.

I finished my degree and then got a job in the Med Center. Instead of getting a house, we stayed in the old Montrose duplex Murphy had lived in for years. I picked out new furniture the same way I'd picked out Murphy's new clothes. We were happy.

Well, sort of.

I'd made a mistake. I'd thought being married to Murphy would be like dating him, only better. I'd never thought he was serious about "being normal," but he was, and I'd already told him that I thought normal was boring. But that wasn't even the real problem. The problem was that Murphy wasn't normal; didn't know how to be.

Also, he had secrets. The one room in the duplex he wouldn't let me redecorate was his office. Sure, every guy likes to have his 'man cave,' but this was a bit more than that. He didn't like me even being in that room... and I didn't like it, either. That room just felt wrong. Even the cats wouldn't go in there... and after a while, I didn't, either.

When he'd first told me his duplex was haunted, I hadn't thought too much of it. Montrose was the Houston equivalent of Haight-Ashbury, and Murphy had lived there pretty much his whole life. I'd always had friends there, and believing in ghosts was pretty par for the course. I'd grown up in the suburbs, which might be why Murphy thought I could coach him on 'normal.' There are no ghosts in Kingwood except the ghosts of lost dreams and opportunities. And I was starting to feel my own dreams dying.

There were other things as well. The more I got to know Murphy, the more I realized no one really knew him at all. His parents were the sweetest people in the world, the total opposite of mine, but nothing they told me about Murphy as a kid matched anything he'd ever said.

I'd already known some of Murphy's old friends and met more, but not a single one of them told the same stories and all the stories had gaps that no one could really fill in. How he had gone from being a part-time bouncer and drug dealer to doing IT consulting was something no one could explain, even Murphy. He just smiled and said, "It's just a knack I have. And it seems to pay pretty well."

We were sitting in what was now our home. The thrift store sofa had been traded out for a suede sectional that Murphy's old gray tabbies were just as inclined to use as a scratching post when no one was looking. The books and records were now on nice new shelves, but they were still the same obscure books and records, now mixed in with some of mine as well. But the wine was the same, and so was Murphy.

Well, sort of.

"It pays well enough," I said, pouring more wine. "Better than my job, for sure."

"Baby, you haven't had one single job in the entire time I've known you that you didn't think sucked."

"Yeah, I suck."

Murphy chuckled. "I wouldn't say that. I think you're pretty awesome."

"I can be a pain in the ass sometimes."

He shrugged. "Most people are. You're still the best thing that ever happened to me."

"I still suck."

"What's wrong? You don't look happy."

"I'm not, Murphy."

"OK, tell me about it."

How do you tell a man who adores you that you're bored out of your mind? How do you tell the charismatic and slightly weird guy that charmed you into marrying him that he's losing the charisma and getting weirder? How do you explain to someone you married because you thought your life was a dead end that marriage is beginning to look like more of the same?

I couldn't... at least not then.

"I've been thinking a lot about what you said the last time we went to see Shannon."

"I say a lot of things. Which thing was this?"

"The thing about how much you like it up there." Shannon Smith had been pretty close to my only friend in high school, but he moved to Alaska about the time I started seeing Murphy. I hadn't expected Murphy to like the Pacific Northwest the first time we went. Add it to the list of things I didn't really know about my husband. He loved it.

"Well, I do. Beats the hell out of Texas."

"Would you ever want to live there?"

"Maybe, would you?"

"I've thought about. Thought about a lot of things."

"Tell me about it."

"I'm really, really not happy. We've got an okay life, but I just don't feel like it's going anywhere. I don't like my job, and even though I love living in Montrose, I feel like it's yuppifying out from under us. As much as you even talk about your job, you don't seem to like it all that much, either. As much as you talk about not liking it here, there're times when I think you're just another Texas good 'ol boy at heart who 'just cain't leave mommah'.

"I feel like we're stuck, and it's making me crazy. When I get crazy, I start thinking crazy things."

Murphy sighed and put his arm around me. "The only person I can't leave is you, baby. And I hardly qualify as a *good 'ol boy*."

"No, you don't. You're actually kind of an asshole."

"Oh, I'm a complete asshole, but I'm not stupid." He stared into the fire and held me. I wondered why he loved me, wondered why I loved him back.

He sighed again and poured us more wine. "I can't really quit my job... but I could maybe take it with me. Figure out a plan, and we can talk. Please tell me you are not talking about Alaska."

I shook my head. "Alaska reminds me of Texas. But Washington's nice. So is Oregon."

"I'm good either way. I just want you to be happy."

"I'll think about it."

six: murphy

Layers within layers, truths within truths. Not all meeting invites arrive via smartphone.

Some arrive via dreams.

I had fallen asleep after the one meeting. No surprise that the other I had expected soon followed.

In my dream, a Thing crouched at my feet and beckoned me. I awakened, and the Thing was still there. It smiled at me crookedly.

"Hail, Jocephus, I assume the boss wants to talk?"

"Indeed," rumbled the Thing. "Much has happened, as you well know."

"I hope we can keep this short," I said. "I need to log into my 'day job' in a few hours."

"Time matters not," said the Thing as it made its way from the end of my sofa to the doors to my outdoor deck. As it approached, the doors opened, and a pearly light that was almost moonlight spilled through. I arose and followed the Thing into the light.

* * *

There are as many tales of The Order's founding as it has names. Some stories trace it back to Atlantis. There's a legend of black-robed men present at Christ's crucifixion claiming to either work for the Sanhedrin or Rome, depending on who you talked to, intimidating and suppressing witnesses to the Death and Resurrection.

Of course, those are damned lies since neither Jesus nor Atlantis ever really happened. The truth, as I know it, is that one day, advisors to

Elizabeth I realized that they had both friends and adversaries in common...and that there were threats to the realm worse than Spain.

The organization founded by Johannes Dee and Francis Walsingham lasts to this day, inspiring legends and half-truths, including intentionally useful disinformation, some of which I wrote. By the time I'd been inducted into The Order, it was pretty close to impossible to distinguish truth from fiction from wishful thinking, then the World Wide Web happened, and it all got a lot worse. Me? I just believe what I've seen with my own eyes, which does not narrow things down nearly as much as you might think.

* * *

The object hovering over the deck of my condo would meet the standard definition of a 'UFO' since all the acronym means to anyone anymore is 'flying saucer.' The top half glinted like silver in the dim light of the new moon peeking through the clouds. The bottom half shone like the full moon itself, lighting my deck bright enough to read by.

Bright enough to see that I had company.

It's not a big deck, but it's big enough for a firepit and some chairs. The pit was glowing with the embers of a fire I hadn't lit. One of the chairs was occupied... by my boss. My real, real boss.

The Order recruits a lot from The Company but not so much the other way around. The reasons why are sometimes strikingly apparent. Evangeia de Lourdes, more or less passes for human, might actually even be more or less human. Certainly, I've known a few redheads with alabaster-white skin and burnished copper hair, not a few of which had high and narrow and somewhat reptilian cheeks or even obliquely angled ice-blue eyes. But the complete package doesn't happen very often, and they aren't usually well over six feet tall. Also, they age, and Evangeia had more or less looked the same for well over twenty years.

She was wearing a pale gray tailored jacket and slacks and a gray silk blouse, boardroom perfect except for the fact that she wasn't wearing any shoes or hose on her long and narrow feet. Balanced on the rim of the firepit was a large mug of a local tea I keep on hand for such occasions. Sitting on a nearby table was a bottle of Benedictine and a shot glass. "I helped myself," she said. "I hope you don't mind." The voice was low-pitched and, as always, also vaguely disturbing.

"No worries." I sat as well. Benedictine and herbal tea sounded disgusting, but it was a cold night. I poured a shot of Benedictine and waited. Jocephus bounded to the deck railing and then to the roof, taking up station and looking like something art thieves had nicked from a cathedral.

I was considering a second shot when she spoke. "How was your meeting with Case?"

I went for the second shot. "About as much fun as you might think. This would be a worst-case scenario even if Case was reporting up to reasonably sane people. Given the current administration, it is much worse than worst case."

"Interesting. Tell me more."

"As always, apologies if I am conveying old information, but here's the deal: an extremely sensitive orbital asset had a very odd and unfortunate encounter with something that wasn't supposed to be there and wound up in the Indian Ocean...more or less intact. As a result, there is a 'situation' in the works that could easily boil up into a Bay of Pigs-level snafu if it isn't properly contained.

"My team has been detailed to handle disinformation and containment. That's all I know. Everything is being handled on a 'need to know' basis. Which brings up an interesting question."

She sipped her tea and shrugged. "By all means."

"Whatever tipped the Archangel Array out of orbit is so much not 'business as usual.' They don't even want to talk about it. So here's the question: As far as The Order is concerned, what's my 'need to know'? I'm finding it pretty unlikely that we're no more informed on this matter than The Company. On the other hand, there are more things in heaven and earth than I have any business dreaming of. If this is one of those cases, I at least need to know that."

The not-quite-human woman who had led my initiation stared at me momentarily in a manner reminiscent of a snake sizing up a mouse. Then she smiled, looking even less human in the process. "Oh, rest assured, dear Horatio, this is as much beyond my philosophy as yours.

"There is a possibility that this... object corresponds to something mentioned in Grandmaster Dee's older writings. Unless you are fluent in Enochian, there is little I could share with you that would make any more sense than what you know already. Interesting that they called it that, by the way."

"I'm sorry?"

"Your 'sensitive orbital asset,' 'Archangel Array' is, at the very least, a name that begs a few questions."

It was my turn to shrug. "In case you hadn't noticed, the people I report to in my 'day job' have some fairly grandiose tendencies."

"True enough."

"As much as I enjoy these little encounters, I'm a lot more useful to everyone concerned if I actually get to sleep every once in a while. You didn't just drop by to ask me about a Company staff meeting, Evangeia."

"I might well have done, Murphy. Your insights and intuitions are more valuable than you realize."

"Spare me. What else is up?"

She stared into the dying embers in the firepit for a long time before replying and continued to stare as she spoke.

"Nothing has been withheld from you as a secret, save those things that remain secret to The Order at large. A greater initiation may well be unfolding for us all. I have a... sense, an intuition, that you will play a role in this. And so I have a favor to ask."

She turned her ice-blue gaze upon me like a weapon. It was all I could do to not flinch from that pitiless stare. "If anything at all unusual or exceptional crosses your path, I need to know. Every oracle I consulted shows you in the midst of this, as well as other things that make even less sense.

"So, you tell me, Murphy: Is there anything I 'need to know'?"

seven: murgenstaern

I am not nearly as impressed with talking monkey progress over the last century or three as they are impressed with it themselves... but I will certainly grant credit where credit is due. Two things, in particular, have impressed me: One is that they have 'advanced' to the point where they are now an existential threat to not only themselves but the majority of the multi-celled species that share their planet. I will be even more

44

impressed if they manage to survive with this capability for another century or so, but prior experience leaves me skeptical this will happen.

The other thing that has impressed me even more is that, if only on an intellectual level and if only among a handful of their number, they have begun to understand the scope and scale of time.

On other occasions when I have relaxed this masquerade that I am one of them, one of the hardest things has been to explain what it means to have existed as a sentient being for the majority of all time... starting with just how much time that involves. It remains really beyond their true comprehension, but at least the educated among them understand that the universe has been around somewhat longer than the 5 or 6 millennia required by their folklore. Perhaps someday, they will understand what it means to have been continually conscious for billions of years (for, of course, I do not sleep). Come that day, and perhaps they might understand the profound loneliness that forms the core of my being. Assuming, again, they do not destroy themselves first.

Of course, my perception and experience of time is no more like a human's than a human's is like unto an ant's. For one thing, I have control over it. As the universe expanded, I contracted, and leaving this place became more difficult; there were millions of years when I found the procession of galaxies across the sky more entertaining than the procession of animals across this particular planet. This changed somewhat once the animals learned to talk and find entertaining ways to butcher one another, but not so much as you might think. Much of the time, I am more inclined than not to hit what humans might currently think of as the 'fast-forward button' in what more or less amounts to my brain.

That is essentially what I did once I agreed to meet Murphy for a beer in a day's time. As the twilight deepened, I felt a moment of something almost like admiration. I could tell that the old monkey was dealing with a severe case of 'fight or flight' syndrome as he casually turned his back and strolled away, particularly severe given that 'fight' was hardly anything approaching a real option.

I waited until he was well out of sight, then made for the trailhead at the back of the park and headed uphill. The clouds that had been gathering since sundown were now shedding a steady drizzle in the thickening darkness. As soon as I was sure I would not be seen, I sped up to a sprint on the winding trail. While I am indifferent to rain, the suit I was wearing less so, and it was one of my favorites.

A few moments later, I was home and, not long after, seated in what I might call the "Thomas Jerome Newton room," were I inclined to have guests. I had gotten a decent bottle from the cellar, made sure the video wall was on autopilot, and then let my time sense drift. I would remember if anything important crossed the screens, but that hardly meant that I needed to pay close attention.

As the sun rose, then moved toward midday, I began to slow my time sense to what passes for normal among humans. I picked out another suit, dressed, and made my way back down the trail. At the appointed time, I was seated at a table in the back of the Lyin' Lamb where I would be certain to see Murphy's entrance. Not long after my own arrival, Murphy appeared as well, got a pint, and joined me.

"Well, cheers, you evil bastard," he said as he dropped into the seat on the other side of the table. "You got me to do something last night I really shouldn't oughta done."

eight: murphy

I'm pretty sure that Evangeia, whatever she really is, is about 90% getting by on looks and intimidation. It's never really worked on me. I was really surprised to find out that there were people in this world, human people, who considered her appearance a turn-on. I'd sooner fuck a snake, myself. As for intimidation, this is pretty far from my first rodeo.

So yeah. I lied to my boss/lodge master, who may or may not be either half space alien or half demon or very possibly a little of both. Also, don't use phrases like 'need to know' with me unless you are prepared to let me make that particular judgment call.

In any case, asking someone who's essentially a CIA/Illuminati double agent if anything 'unusual' has happened lately involves a pretty fair number of sweeping assumptions.

I had poured myself another shot of Benedictine as the inhumanly pretty lady and her pet golem/gargoyle rode a moonbeam back into her personal flying saucer, which then disappeared with neither sound nor optical effects worth mentioning. Then I crashed hard. Even though I'd had problems with insomnia ever since Caroline left, this was one occasion when I slept like a baby.

The next day went pretty much to plan as far as The Job was concerned. By the end of my shift, my offshore teams had put out enough disinformation that even anyone who had been tracking Archangel Array when it went down was probably wondering what had really happened. Meanwhile, my stateside team had managed to locate anyone who might have been foolish enough to leak the actual telemetry data and pass their coordinates onto the appropriate parties to be 'neutralized' in various ways.

In almost no time at all, it was quitting time. And time for a few decisions.

Certainly, not keeping the appointment had crossed my mind...but I knew that wasn't really an option. Evangeia's vague references to 'oracles' had only confirmed my own intuition. Whatever had happened to the Archangel Array was far more The Order's business than The Company's.

I remained my own Devil's Advocate on the question of who or what Murgenstaern really was. He could even be human, for all I really knew. But he either knew or thought he knew what had actually brought down the Array, and Evangeia's veiled comments confirmed it was nothing mundane.

And if Murgenstaern was anything close to what he claimed, he was probably the most fluent speaker of 'Enochian' on the entire planet.

The possibility that this could all be some sort of trap remained not unlikely. I'm not that particularly important in either The Company or The Order, but there are a few folks out there from back in the day who wouldn't mind terribly if I turned up dead or worse. Even though it was mostly a placebo to paranoia, I decided to dress for the occasion, mixing a bit of tactical field gear with some of my old punk-era leather that (I'm proud to say) still fits.

Caroline probably would've made fun of me, but I should probably stop thinking about what Caroline might think about any damned thing. For a moment, I considered the sheer impossibility of explaining any of this to her. Then, I compartmentalized and moved on to the next thing.

'Compartmentalize': It's something I've done most of my life, something I started taking to an extreme after my wife left me. When it's time to do The Job, that's what I do, without a single thought spared for anyone or anything else. When it's time to do The Order's bidding, I do that. When it's time to drink, I drink. When it's time to sleep, I do my best. I compartmentalize and do everything possible to leave as little time as possible for the compartment labeled 'grieve over losing my wife.'

It's not a perfect approach, but it works. I'm still alive, and I still have a job. I still have a home and a life. It's still the home and life I made for her...But there's nothing I can do about that.

Now I had a new compartment, and I wasn't sure what to call it. 'Consorting with Satan' and 'trying to save the world' were both choices that came to mind, but so did 'killing time until time gets around to killing me.' The presumption that I still cared enough about the world to save it was maybe even a bigger presumption than taking at face value a guy claiming to be Lucifer.

As a final touch, I stuffed my old gray paisley scarf down the front of the jacket. Instead of walking to the Lamb, I decided to drive. My old Porsche is like my old leather jacket, or like me, I suppose. Beat up and not so shiny and definitely seen better days. But everything works, and 'shiny' is overrated. Refusing to put the top up in anything less than a downpour had fubar'd the upholstery. Dyeing it black and applying black duct tape to the busted seams had fixed things as far as I was concerned.

It was a short drive to The Lamb, made shorter by the fact I still drive like a guy from Texas. The place was already filling up by the time I got there. Luckily, Murgenstaern had beat me there and grabbed a table in the back where we could talk without an audience.

I grabbed a pint and made my way back. He was watching the Seahawks administer a beatdown to the 49ers on the big screen in the front of the bar like he actually gave a shit, which maybe he did, for all I knew. I asked my instincts again if he was any more or less human than, say, Evangeia.

49

The answer remained "probably less." I wasn't inducted into The Order for psychic ability. I've picked up a few bits of Chaos Magick over the years, but any random half-dozen folks at a Throbbing Gristle tribute show are probably better than I am. But I trust my instincts and my intuition. At the end of the day, they're all I've got.

"Well, cheers, you evil bastard," I said, taking the other seat. "You got me to do something last night I really shouldn't oughta done."

He glanced down from the TV. As soon as he stopped pretending to watch the game, he stopped pretending to be human or, at least, normal. "Good to see you as well, Murphy. By all means, tell me more unless the lapse in question is a personal matter."

"Oh, no. Quite professional." I took a long drag on my beer. "I lied to someone who is pretty much capable of everything they say about you. Granted, it was just a lie of omission...but that ain't gonna save my ass if shit goes south."

He shrugged. "If shit well and truly 'goes south,' I could wind up the only fully sentient biped on this planet. What happened?"

"Not that much. I just neglected to tell my boss, my real boss, about my new drinking buddy, Satan himself, when I was asked if I had noticed anything 'unusual' lately."

"Sounds like a small enough matter. And I am not Satan."

"You weren't there. As for the 'Satan' wisecrack, what difference does it make? You aren't 'Lucifer' either, in any meaningful sense."

It wasn't a long pause, but it was definitely there. "Only in ways that are meaningful to me."

"And if I'm real lucky, I might even live long enough to understand or appreciate any of that. What're you drinking, by the way?"

"Boneyard, actually."

"Appropriate. I'm grabbing another round, and then it's time to 'talk shop,' old son."

Getting another round gave me a moment to think about where I wanted to take this. The problem with depending on instinct and intuition is that a lot of the time, you wind up being shit for advance planning. On the other hand, sometimes stuff works out anyway.

By the time I made it back with a couple of fresh pints, I'd thought things through as far as maybe staying alive for another day or two. "So," I said. "How about we skip ahead to the part about making whatever it is I'm supposed to be doing worth my while? Anything I need to sign in my own blood?"

"What I have in mind may or may not require shed blood, but I think we can dispense with wasting any on signed agreements. As for your compensation, if this works, it is my fond hope to be done with this place... this planet. You are welcome to amuse yourself as you please with whatever I leave behind here, assuming your various employers don't take it from you."

I'd gotten similar pitches in various parts of Central America back in the day. I'd never particularly cared for it back then, either. "Fine. I wind up wealthy beyond my wildest dreams, assuming I don't wind up in small bloody bits. What I really want is probably beyond even your ability to grant. We can talk about it later. You said you needed my help. Let's talk about that. And just so we understand each other, if anything is on a 'need to know' basis, I'm outta here as soon as I'm done with this beer."

"Fair enough, although some of what I tell you must be taken at my word."

"That'll work... for now."

"Best I start at the beginning."

"Good thing I got another round."

nine: murgenstaern

Genesis and astrophysics are not as out of alignment as they are frequently thought to be once you make allowances for differences in languages and perspective, at least the parts I know about. I was willed into being sometime between the Big Bang and the creation of space. There were many of us. Beings of pure energy created solely to hear and carry out what might be described as 'the word of God.' Angels, in other words.

We numbered many, though not infinite, and through our ministrations, the stars and galaxies formed. We watched the universe expand and take shape.

A thing we had not expected happened as the universe expanded. God remained at the center of what God had wrought. We could not. The face of God grew more distant, the voice of God more faint.

Also, we grew smaller. Or rather, stayed the same.

Some remained closer to the center of the cosmos and grew greater from their proximity to the Power and the Glory. Others remained true to their purpose as messengers and ministers of The Plan as they knew it, remaining in the periphery of the expanding universe to shape the course of that expansion. As time and space grew, our ability to move within it lessened. The effort of even traversing a mere galaxy became great. Then, even to move between solar systems exceeded us.

Then, finally, those of us who had chosen to remain and carry out The Word became as planet-bound as the creatures we had shepherded into existence in obedience to that Word.

I call myself "Morningstar," among other reasons, in remembrance of the bright morning of Creation. Whatever I chose to resemble, at my core, I am a piece of that bright morning, a conscious singularity.

By the time humankind arose from the muck, the time I could have left this world was drawing to a close. I chose to stay, feeling that sentience arising from mere matter must be what The Master intended all along. And so here I remain.

But here is the thing humans fail to understand about the depths of time. Given enough time, almost anything is possible. Monkeys can learn to talk and yield the fire of Creation. Rifts can occur in an ever-expanding cosmos, granting access to... elsewhere.

When my kind was created, other things were created as well. Less than angels, but more than mere matter. Those shards of my birth matrix continued to travel outward, though not as angels fly. Over enough time, such a shard might even overtake a small planet in the outer cosmos.

Were I to merge my inner being with such a thing, I would grow great again. Not so great as to be a shaper of galaxies, but great enough to travel among them. Perhaps even to go home.

I had known that, in time, such a thing might come within my grasp. Sometimes, patience pays.

"So, does this thing have a name?" It had taken more than a round, of course. Retelling Genesis from a first-person perspective isn't a particularly quick or easy affair, even given the huge chunks of material Murgenstaern had certainly skipped over.

"None in any human tongue. Why would it?"

"Point taken. What does it look like?"

"Like myself, it could look like almost anything. Given where it has been for most of time, it probably looks...like a rock, more than not. It is a leftover piece of the stuff God used to make angels. Call it a Seraphim Stone."

"Nice. OK, 'Seraphim Stone' it is. So here's another question. How are you so sure of what this thing is? I'm tapped into some pretty serious insider sources, and if any of them have a clue, they are keeping it pretty close to home."

"I am sure you have little more trust for any of your various employers than I do, but it doesn't matter. I know that the Stone is here. It calls to me. I hear it every bit as much as I once heard the voice of The Almighty."

"This would be the part where I have to take you at your word, right?"

"One such, to be sure."

"Hopefully, there will not be many. Can we now, finally, talk about what it is you need me to do?"

"Very little, really. I need you to help me gain access to wherever The Stone winds up."

I had sort of seen it coming. "In which case, you are out of luck, old son."

"How so?"

"Let's start with the 'wherever it winds up' part. The Archangel Array, along with your mcguffin, was successfully retrieved from the Indian Ocean earlier today by a U.S. naval task force. There was never any real doubt of that outcome. I don't have a high enough security clearance to know exactly what happened after that, but I have enough institutional knowledge to fill in the gaps.

Right now, your Seraphim Stone and the Archangel Array wreckage are under extreme lock and key, probably on an aircraft carrier underway to a U.S. airbase, probably Diego Garcia.

"What happens after that has a lot to do with just how much your Seraphim Stone really looks like a rock. If the incident forensics team finds even a trace of anything that doesn't look 'like a rock, more or less,' it's going to get airlifted straight to Nevada."

"Area 51?"

I laughed. "For an angelic being, you have some quaint and misinformed notions. Area 51, Area 52, hell, for all I know, they've trotted out an 'Area 53' by now. That's all misdirection. But I do know that any expert analysis of a suspected extraterrestrial organism or artifact is going to take place at one of several high-security facilities in the less populated parts of Nevada, and that's just assuming this remains 'Company' business."

I was beginning to get a sense of how to 'read' Murgenstaern. For the most part, his 'human suit' was damned near perfect. But when something got his attention, he would forget to act human. When something really got his attention, he essentially turned to stone. He turned into a statue for a brief moment before speaking.

"I assume you refer to what you describe as your 'real' employers."

"Correct. I am hardly the only mole The Order has embedded within the U.S. shadow government. Area Fifty Whatever is so infiltrated that it might as well be considered a joint operation. And that's where it gets a bit more interesting… but still hypothetical."

"How so?"

This was not gonna be fun, but I couldn't see a way around it. "I can't help you, Murgenstaern. All the riches in the world or whatever you were planning to offer me is of no use if I'm dead, which is how I will wind up if I take any unauthorized field trips to Nevada, much less the Indian Ocean."

"How do you wind up dead?"

"Unlike you, I'm going to wind up that way no matter what. The way I wind up that way in a hurry is by fucking with my employers. Let's start with my 'day job.' Do you really think I get to just 'phone in' a lead role as an intel analyst from some random location in the Pacific Northwest? People like me usually work in a damned dungeon where you don't even go to the pisser without your security badge and occasionally get strip-searched when you go home for the day. I had to pull in a lot of markers for this, had to make some serious promises, and had to agree to some serious conditions.

"When I was still married, my wife tried to get the cable company to add some movie channels as a 'surprise.' Luckily, Caroline was never any damned good at keeping secrets. Otherwise, we would've all gotten a surprise the moment a local cable company tech tried to touch my damned modem.

"I don't know for sure that my house would get blown up if I missed work under unusual circumstances, but I'm not inclined to find out. If I want time off, I have to ask for it months in advance. There is spyware on my phone that I know about, including stuff I'm not supposed to know about, and probably more stuff that I don't know about. Post-Snowden, the measures adopted to keep people like me in line got very serious. Given the current administration, I keep my head down and my nose clean."

"Does not your affiliation with The Order affect any of this?"

I guess a transcendental being can get by on raw power in a state of ignorance. Must be nice.

"Yeah, it makes things a damned sight more complicated. The Order doesn't need any of that crap to keep me on a short leash. They actually respect my privacy one helluva lot more than The Company does, but the consequences of going rogue on them would make for a very entertaining and very short supernatural horror flick.

"At some point, I would love to find out what you really know and what you are really capable of, assuming we continue to have the occasional beer together and you were just joking about making me disappear. But, as far as helping you break into a highly secured facility to get some thingamajig that's going to get you off this planet, I don't know who the hell you think you're talking to. I'm just a broken-down old fuck with an interesting history and a collection of bad life choices.

"I'm sure a lot of people would want to read something deeper into the coincidence of us meeting, including the people I'm lying to about having even met you. Hell, they don't believe anything is a 'coincidence,' but I'm beginning to think it may be exactly that."

Another statue moment, and then the statue spoke. "There are those who say that everything happens for a reason."

I laughed. "If you are one of them, then you have spent the better part of eternity learning nothing. My wife, sorry, ex-wife, believes crap like that, believes that it was somehow 'fate' that she'd wind up on the other side of the country engaged to some asshat she met in some bar."

I laughed again. It even sounded nasty to me, but I couldn't help it. "Good-looking women hanging out in bars get hooked up, just like free radicals wind up forming molecules. It ain't fate; it's physics.

"As for your 'Seraphim Stone,' I just don't see any urgency here. It's been around forever and so have you. The way things are going, you can just wait a century, snag it from the wreckage after humanity has finished committing suicide, and be on your way. Hell, that's what I'd do."

It had taken a few beers to get to this point, and I'd been leaning toward double and triple IPAs. But I truly and honestly no longer gave a shit. About anything, really. I should've known, though, that he wasn't going to let me off the hook that easy. After a few moments of statue-like stillness, he spoke.

"Your analysis is correct on almost all points, with two important exceptions. One is that there is, in fact, some urgency here that will not await the collapse of your civilization. The other is that the impediments to aiding me you have mentioned are all matters with which I can assist, at least as far as concerns your 'day job.'

"The Order is a different matter, although I have some means of dealing with them, as well as some history with them, as well as with those they oppose. Any urgency here comes from that history.

"I suppose I have been operating on a 'need to know' basis. Your need just escalated. Time I told you a few things about your Order, as well as a few things about me."

Part 3: Discretion

one: murgenstaern

No living creature on this planet ever has or ever could bear witness to my true nature. Luckily, the matter accretes to me. By the time it mattered what that matter looked like, I had become quite adept at shaping it to suit my needs.

Once this had become my place of exile, it had become my habit to pass among humans as one of their own. Call it discretion, if you will. I could appear among them as a God if I liked and have done so on occasion. But it never turns out well for the humans, or me, given that I hate having to move.

Imagine my dismay when I discovered I was not the only such imposter.

I knew they were not other angels. The light of Creation cannot be hidden from those who contain that light as well. But equally evident was that they were no more human than I.

They were among those who first began to appear after the rifts opened. It was no coincidence.

The continued expansion of the universe had opened holes in its fundamental fabric, and things from Elsewhere had crept in. I find it unimaginable that this was not part of God's plan, but we don't talk anymore, so really I cannot say.

I had no idea what they were at that time, and, in many ways, I know little more now. Others later followed through the rifts, and factions among them formed various alliances with humans. The group that calls itself "The Order" is one among these.

I had believed myself invisible to all of these Others until the day a group attempted to ambush me and drag me into a portal to their Elsewhere. I learned that day how better to disguise myself. They learned that day that a diminished archangel... is still an archangel.

The Stones are of the nature of angels, but they are not angels. Whatever these Others might wish to do in their universe with pieces of this universe's early creation concerns me not at all, although I have a few guesses. But they are not welcome to the piece that's me. Or the piece that frees me from this prison.

two: murphy

We were no longer in The Lamb. I'd gotten a growler and a couple of glasses. We were sitting in the back of the same little park we'd wound up in the previous night. It made as much sense as anything else I'd done lately.

"Nonhumans in human disguise don't narrow things down by much. Do you know who they were?"

Murgenstaern had again opted to sit on the picnic table. I had found an abandoned lawn chair and was sitting with my feet propped on the table. The growler sat between us. We each had a glass.

He shook his head. "I wished to set an example for any Others who might consider attempting such a thing."

"You made them 'disappear'?"

"Something on that order. Too little remained for any meaningful analysis."

"But you think whoever it was, or someone like them, is still here on Earth?"

"It is a risk I cannot afford to take. That's why I am declining your helpful suggestion that I simply let the Stone remain warehoused until after the impending collapse of current human civilization, and that is why I need your help."

"I'm still waiting," I said, "to hear the part about how you can disarm my booby-trapped modem and the other 'impediments,' as you call them, to joining you on a road trip. I'm also waiting for the part about why I want to, particularly if I wind up crossing The Order in the process."

"The 'why' part is fairly simple, and as I have said, I have resources that could enable you to live out the rest of your life very comfortably. Resources I will no longer need, resources that far exceed anything either The Order or The Company will ever share with you, should you spend your remaining days at their bidding.

"The 'how' part is a little more complicated. This body you are having a beer with is essentially a puppet the 'real me' operates from within by remote control. Telekinesis, if you like. The various toys employed by your 'day job' to ensure your obedience are far less complex than my 'puppet.' I need only physical proximity to bend them to my will."

"Okay," I said. "Now, how about the part where we actually get there? Do you sprout wings and fly to the Indian Ocean? Or do your 'resources' include a private jet or two?"

"I can transport myself anywhere on the face of this planet. Transporting you as well to the far side of the world would be somewhat difficult, but not necessary. Your prediction that the Seraphim Stone would be moved is coming true. It is moving and moving this way."

"I still haven't said I'd help you."

"No, but neither have you said you would not. You have only pointed out reasons why you could not. I do not need an answer now, but I will need one soon. If you chose not to aid me, I will take you at your word and seek other options."

"You have other options?"

"No good ones, nor am I as convinced as you there is nothing more to our meeting than coincidence. But I cannot and will not compel you into this against your will. I would like to ask you another question, though."

"Sure," I said, pouring another beer. "Ask away"

"I do not believe this is the life you wanted. You are a bitter, angry, and lonely man. You are an adept who pretends to be a spy who pretends to be ordinary, and yet none of those things are what you truly are. If not this, what? What do you propose to do with what remains of your life?"

It was the same question I'd been asking myself ever since I'd watched Caroline walk away in search of a new life, the question that kept me awake on the nights the meds and the booze weren't enough to keep me asleep.

I never had a 'plan B.' I'm not good at 'plan B.' I'd put my heart and soul and every resource I'd had into the one plan of having a life with Caroline. I'd kept my job at the cost of my career and pushed my real job as far out of my life as I could. By the time Caroline decided life here and life with me wasn't what she wanted after all, I had painted myself into a corner. Worse yet, I'd gotten old.

Part of the reason I'd been willing to leave behind everything and everyone else I had ever known or loved, leave Texas, and start over again in the Northwest was because I knew it was the one chance I'd ever have and that I'd spend the rest of my life regretting not doing it.

The other part was that I was literally willing to face down demons for Caroline. Too bad I could never tell her. All I could tell her was that I loved her. Too bad that wasn't enough.

"I don't have a good answer for that," I told Murgenstaern, "and I don't have an answer to your proposition, either, at least not right this minute. I have no idea what else I want to do. There are times when I feel like I'm dead already and this is just some sort of crappy afterlife.

"Assuming otherwise that I am still alive and want to stay that way, the smartest thing I can possibly do is leave here right now while I'm still marginally sober enough to get home and find a new watering hole for a while.

"The stupidest thing I could do would be to take your gig without some serious proof that you can deliver on one damned thing you've offered.

"The second stupidest thing I could do, and God help me, I'm considering it, is to ask for that serious proof. I'm one of the goddam fucking Men in Black, dude. You can tell me you're a fallen angel from the center of the universe without getting laughed at. Consider it a professional courtesy. But if you expect me to risk what's left of my career as well as my one and only puny human life, you need to throw down, old son. Show me a miracle or two, something better than the run-of-the-mill magick I've used and had used on me for the last twenty years. If it's impressive enough, we'll talk."

I jumped to my feet. A little unsteady, but I've been worse.

"You can have the rest of the beer. Just be sure to return the growler and the glasses. You can even keep the deposit."

Murgenstaern shook his head. "Take it with you. But I agree with you that should not drink more if you are planning to drive home."

I threw the glasses and the growler in the bag they'd given me at the bar. "I'm good, but your concern is duly noted."

"When shall we meet again?"

"You figure it out, you get in touch. Text me, or send over a sasquatch with an engraved gold tablet. Impressive, remember? I'm out. Need me to drop you off anywhere?"

He shook his head again. "Do try to be careful. I shall consider your words. I will be in touch."

"Marvelous. Later, dude."

* * *

The walk back to the parking lot didn't sober me up as much as I'd hoped it would, but it sobered me up enough to realize that my usual route home was a busier street than I felt like dealing with. I was a little startled to find The Lamb closed when I got there. I'd been hanging out with Murgenstaern a lot longer than I'd realized. Well, it wouldn't be the first time I'd ever logged in for work with a hangover, not by a long shot.

I threw the bag with the growler in the back of the Porsche and eased my way out of the parking lot, back the way I'd come. Not surprisingly, Murgenstaern was no longer there when I drove past the park.

From there, the road wound up the side of the mountain, then down again. Yeah, I was taking the curves a little fast.

But I would've been fucked at any speed when the tire blew.

The car spun through a railing and pitched forward into a ravine. The bag with the growler and glasses flew ahead from the back seat. It occurred to me that I was going to lose the deposit on the growler.

three: caroline

We talked it back and forth for a year. In some ways, things got better; in some ways, worse. But we finally made a decision. Once I finished my degree, we'd leave. Yeah, I'd gone back to school. It was the one thing I was really good at, and another Masters might help me land a new job.

Having a goal helped me. I was still married to a charming older man with a mysterious past, but at least the present was less mysterious, and I could convince myself there was a future.

We still traveled a lot when we could, but more and more of our vacations focused on parts of the Northwest I could talk Murphy into moving to. I'd given up on getting him to go much of anywhere else. He flatly did not want to go to South or Central America and would not say why. I'd think about the rumors I'd heard about him... and decided I didn't want to know.

It really wasn't a bad life. I worked at a hospital in the Texas Medical Center, Murphy worked in an office building in downtown Houston. Sometimes, one of us would hop on the light rail line between the two and meet somewhere for lunch or happy hour.

I got to meet some of Murphy's coworkers. They seemed like any other group of IT people you'd run into in downtown, except for the fact that when they 'talked shop,' it was even more incomprehensible than usual. And they never never invited anyone up to their office.

They were nice, though, and they all seemed to like Murphy, even though the "Murphy" they talked about didn't sound very much like the one his old friends talked about or even the one I thought I knew.

"You know Colvin Case has a big 'ol man-crush on you, right?" We were sitting on the patio watching the sunset. It was a nice, private space behind Murphy's duplex facing away from the street. It was also a lush little private jungle where the cats could stalk lizards and birds. It was a warm evening, warm enough to switch from our usual red wine to a chilled bottle of something white and slightly fizzy.

Murphy laughed. "The only thing Case has a crush on is his career. You know he's going to wind up being my boss, right?"

"I'm surprised they didn't offer it to you."

"They did. I turned it down."

"When did this happen?"

"A couple of months ago."

"Nice of you to say something."

"What's to say?" Murphy refreshed our glasses. "We had already made other plans that involve going the opposite direction."

"Opposite direction?"

"Well, yeah, Case is going to have to relocate to the main office in Baltimore."

"I wouldn't mind living in Baltimore."

"I thought you wanted to go live in the Northwest so you could hang out with Shannon." Murphy looked confused and exasperated. But not as exasperated as I was.

"I just want to get out of here. I don't want to be some failure who spends the rest of their life in the city they grew up in."

"You just described most of my friends, and you pretty much just described me."

There was a long silence while I tried to figure out a way to say I was sorry when I really wasn't, or if I even wanted to. Then Murphy broke the silence.

"Wow," he said. "Would you look at that," and pointed into the sky.

I looked. A bright light was descending through the twilight. "A shooting star," I said. "Cool."

"Make a wish if you haven't already."

"That's weird. It looked like it changed directions."

"That's been known to happen," Murphy said. "Which way is it going?"

"Toward the airport, North, I guess."

"Maybe it's an omen. Maybe that's where we should be going as well."

I took a deep breath. Half the time I got mad at him, I wasn't really sure why, I wasn't even sure if he was really why I was mad. "Great timing," I said.

"How so?"

"It sure changed the subject."

An odd smile crossed Murphy's face. "If I could arrange things like that, we could pretty much live anywhere we wanted."

"If you could 'arrange things like that,' you could probably just make me be happy anywhere you wanted to be."

The smile fell. "It ain't that simple, baby. Sometimes I wish it was."

four: murphy

"I was just kidding," I said as the world came back into focus. "Still, the engraved gold tablet would've been a nice touch."

"No need and no time," Murgenstaern replied. "For this is no messenger of mine. I could still fabricate the tablet if you remain unimpressed."

"Fuck both you guys," said the sasquatch.

I was sitting in an extremely comfortable chair that looked like it had been appropriated from a high-end gentleman's club or the United Emirates airport lounge. Murgenstaern was similarly seated not far away. The sasquatch was sitting a few yards away, crosslegged on the floor. He didn't have much choice in the matter, given that there was a metal collar around his neck attached to the floor by way of four extremely heavy chains. More chains bound his wrists. Behind him, I could see my old Porsche. Except for the blown tire, it was far more intact than it had any business being. So was I.

There wasn't much else in the room, which was a hundred feet or so across and appeared to be hewn from solid rock. Sunlight streamed in from skylights in a distant ceiling. Other, smaller rooms were on the periphery. One of them was full of flat-panel TVs. Another appeared to be full of racks of men's suits.

The expected impact with the ravine floor simply... never happened. The Porsche had continued to fall through increasing blackness, slowed, and then stopped. At some point, the engine and headlights had shut off. Turning the lights back on had crossed my mind, as well as a few other things I'd wished I'd thought of sooner. But I didn't seem to be dead, and staying that way was beginning to seem like a good idea. As quietly as I could manage, I made my way into the back seat. It had never been intended as something a guy my size could bunk down in, but I managed anyway.

A flashlight and a water bottle were left in the seat pockets from a hike a few weeks earlier. I drained the bottle and made sure the flashlight was where I could find it. Then I took a nap.

Really, what else was I going to do? Wherever I was, it was dead silent and could be anywhere. I had also been drunk enough to get myself in this spot, whatever the hell it was, in the first place. If someone or something wanted me dead, someone or something (maybe the same someone/something) had taken extraordinary measures to keep me above room temperature, at least temporarily.

Floundering around drunk with a flashlight was an option. So was sobering up and waiting for someone/something to make the next move.

Regaining consciousness under present circumstances wasn't exactly what I had expected, but neither was it far removed. "Got any water?" I asked. "I'm still kinda dehydrated."

Murgenstaern nodded. "To your right." An end table I hadn't noticed previously held an ice bucket. In the bucket was the water bottle I'd drained before passing out, apparently refilled.

"Thanks." The cold, clean water was the best thing I'd had in a long time. I drained half the bottle in one pass. "So, how long was I out? Am I a suspected defector at this point, or merely homeless?"

"Neither," Murgenstaern replied. "I took the liberty of disarming your modem as previously offered and turned on the out-of-office message on your computer. I also fed your cats."

"I don't recall offering up either my home address or my spare key."

"Your address is on your driver's license, which happens to be in your wallet between an expired health club membership card and a credit card. I believe I previously mentioned having senses you do not, as well as abilities sufficient to disarming your home security system and the safeguards built into your VPN. I hardly need to point out that having your computer password written on a post-it note affixed to your monitor is something your employers would not appreciate."

I shrugged. "I live alone, and there's nothing simple about any of my security systems. OK, I'm impressed. Any lingering doubts about you being a baseline human with an interesting psychosis have pretty much gone out the window. That still doesn't make you a fallen angel, but William of Occam would probably be arguing in favor of it right about now.

"What about him?" I said, nodding in the sasquatch's direction.

"Fuck both you guys," said the sasquatch.

"Limited vocabulary notwithstanding, he's fairly enterprising, if not quite a credit to his species. He is largely to thank for your present circumstances." Murgenstaern gestured, and a steel utility table rolled into view from one of the side rooms. Sitting on top of it was a rifle. It wasn't the first time I'd ever seen someone use TK, but it was the first time I'd seen Murgenstaern do so. Interesting, if no longer surprising.

"I became aware of his presence not long after you and I parted ways last night," Murgenstaern continued. "His people rarely hunt in this part of The Northwest anymore and, to the best of my awareness, do not do so with rifles. He followed you back to the Lyin' Lamb and continued to follow you once you retrieved your vehicle to head home.

"While he was stalking you, I stalked him. It was actually fortunate that he shot out your tire at the place where your 'accident' occurred since it happens to be directly above this place." Murgenstaern gestured outward with raised palms. "One of my homes, as I suspect you suspect already."

I nodded. It looked more like recent depictions of Bruce Wayne's man cave than anyone's idea of a home, but it fits the profile.

"The entrance at the bottom of that ravine has not been used in a long time, but it remains serviceable. I used it to lower you and your vehicle to this chamber then restrained our friend here. The rest, you largely know."

"Don't think me ungrateful, but why'd you let him shoot my car?"

"I had to be sure of his intentions," Murgenstaern said. "Members of your order claim the ability to read minds, but I have no such ability of my own. My senses, though acute, are entirely physical. I would not have permitted you to be injured in any event. I do still have need of you."

"We can talk about that later," I said. "What about this guy?"

"I think a few questions are in order, after which he can be turned over to his people to deal with as they see fit, after which we most certainly need to talk."

"Fuck both you guys," said the sasquatch.

five: murgenstaern

My fondness for various fermented and distilled beverages has entirely to do with an appreciation of taste, scent, and other factors. The physical component of my masquerade resembles a human being as closely as my abilities permit, but it does not become intoxicated. My true self, needless to say, is far beyond such things.

I had planned, in any event, to ensure Murphy's impaired abilities did not interfere with his return home. I had told him the truth when I told him that my other options for gaining access to the Seraphim Stone were few and poorer. Close to nonexistent, really. I also continued to wonder just how much I could truly consider the discovery of someone with Murphy's credentials in what amounted to my backyard as a 'coincidence.' His associates in The Order, particularly the less human among them, would likely consider it nothing of the kind.

I had also told Murphy the truth when I told him that helping me or not was utterly a matter of his own free will...but I also knew that he'd already made his decision. No, I cannot read minds, but I have been observing humankind for longer than they have been able to observe themselves.

Although I remain somewhat baffled by human mating customs and rituals, I like to think that I understand and am capable of love. Grief over love's loss, I surely understand. What else truly animates me after all other than my own grief and loneliness? I do not believe it is possible for even me to destroy myself, but did I not hold out the hope of ending my exile any time before the end of time itself, I might well have attempted it long ago.

Murphy was as much animated by grief over his failed marriage as I ever had been over losing the voice and vision of God, easily capable of destroying himself, and further marked with a guilt he may not have even realized he had. Still, I realized, guilty that his present state might well have been his own doing, wittingly or not. While not actively seeking to end his own existence, it was evident to me that he was exerting the barest minimum of effort toward his own self-preservation.

I had also spoken truth when I offered to leave in Murphy's hands the various things I had accumulated over the long centuries of my masquerade among humans, as well as when I cautioned him his various masters would likely seize these things, given the chance. I am not sure whether I would be considered 'wealthy' by human standards or not. With less than human appetites and more than human abilities, my holdings barely extend past what I require for my own entertainment and the needs of my masquerade. But even this small one of my homes I had revealed to him was far more than Murphy would ever receive from those he had chosen to serve. If he was prepared to risk his small mortal life in my service, he was welcome to it all.

I had been surprised to see one of the Forest Folk stalking Murphy, far less one armed with a rifle. The beings known locally as 'Sasquatch' were among those who had appeared from Elsewhere when the expanding universe grew thin spots.

Neither beasts nor humans they were entirely capable of concealing themselves. Unlike the humans they somewhat resembled, they were entirely capable of restricting their number to what the forest could support and had neither need for nor interest in human technology. Someone had corrupted this one, and he was going to pay for it. His people have no laws as such but believe very strongly in their customs. He was in violation of several.

His attempt at engineering an automobile accident had simplified matters for me as well as provide an opportunity to cement Murphy's recruitment. I had ascended to the top of what I like to think of as 'my mountain,' from which I could view every inch of the winding road Murphy had chosen, as well as track his pursuer. Although I need close proximity for fine control, it was no challenge for me to reach out with my mind to lower Murphy's vehicle into my home, nor lower myself to the ravine's edge as I did so. The shooter attempted to leave the scene of the crime. I reached out with my mind and prevented that as well.

74

Murphy's decision to pass out in the back of his car was yet another opportunity I put to good use. Having restrained his assailant, I had plenty of time to ensure that Murphy's house would not be blown to rubble before his return, as well as feed his cats and turn on his out-of-office message. He was still going to be in trouble with his 'day job,' but as Murphy himself would say, "That's what happens when you get shithammered on a school night." At least he would be alive to make his excuses.

The sky was beginning to lighten as I returned to my own home, necessitating a somewhat more discreet approach than simply levitating over the top of a mountain or sprinting at high speed across mountain trails. At least there was no rain, for a change.

The sasquatch glowered upon my return and said nothing. I had not been gentle when restraining him. I then sat in the chair across from the one Murphy slumbered in and waited for him to regain consciousness while I considered the next steps.

six: murphy

"Actually," Murgenstaern said to the sasquatch, "given my understanding of such things, you're the one who's fucked. To paraphrase one of my favorite movies, say 'fuck' one more time."

I don't know if the sasquatch caught the Pulp Fiction reference or not, but he caught the tone in Murgenstaern's voice, and caught himself just ahead of a very unwise repetition.

Murgenstaern's 'human suit' was turned all the way up now. He sounded and acted as human as he had the first time I'd ever met him, two extremely busy days ago. But the role he was playing now wasn't 'traveling computer salesman.' I sipped some more water and sat up in my chair. This was going to be interesting.

"You're going back North once we're done here." Murgenstaern was now circling the prisoner, who had essentially been hog-tied with logging chains. "But first, you're answering a couple of questions. I'll make sure there's enough of you left to face justice. Anything past that is entirely up to you."

"You don't scare me." Sasquatches aren't apes. They also aren't human. They're from somewhere else where humans didn't happen. Now they're here. Like the Dutch, they learn English from American TV. Which means that when they're not talking among themselves, they sound just like anyone else in the Pacific Northwest.

"In that case, you are even stupider than you look." Murgenstaern made a gesture not unlike hailing a cab. The 'squatch levitated as far as the chains between its neck and the floor permitted, which wasn't very far. Then, the steel collar around its neck made a creaking sound as it grew tighter. "A little hard to tell someone to fuck themselves if you can't breathe... isn't it?"

After not quite a minute, the creaking and the levitation both stopped...and the sasquatch apparently could once again breathe.

"I could do this all day," Murgenstaern said. "I suspect the same is not true of you. Can we talk?"

The sasquatch nodded as much as its anatomy and restraints permitted. "What do you want to know?" it asked once it could talk again.

"I want to know who you are working for and why they are using you to put a hit on my friend here."

The pause was so long that I expected to see the levitation trick again. "The little guys," he finally said.

"What 'little guys'?"

"You know, the little gray guys with the fucked-up eyes. Them." The Sasquatch rolled his eyes in the general direction of outer space.

"Okay, let's say I believe you. Why?"

The sasquatch shrugged. English isn't the only thing they learn from TV. "Ask them. I got no idea. I don't think they like your buddy... or maybe they don't like who he works for."

"And what the hell would you know about that?" I said.

He glared at me. "I know what was over your house two days ago. Nice ride."

I laughed. "Ever been in one?" The sasquatch just glared.

Murgenstaern jumped in again. I'm not sure which of us was the good cop and which one was the bad cop, given that I felt like strangling the bastard myself. "We're almost done here," he said. "I want to know what your instructions were and when you got them. I also want to know when you got here. If you've been watching my friend's house, you didn't just hit town."

It was the sasquatch's turn to laugh. It didn't sound like American TV or even human. "I've been here a week. The little gray dudes made me a job offer and gave me a ride down here. When I told them who your buddy was working for, they changed the deal and upped the offer. They wanted him out of the picture, wanted it to either look like human-on-human violence or an accident."

"What was the original offer? They just wanted you to watch him?"

The sasquatch laughed again. "The original offer didn't have shit to do with him. They sent me down here to watch you."

seven: caroline

While I was completing my degree, Murphy's mom and dad both passed away, one from pneumonia, the other from a broken heart. Murphy had almost nothing to say at the funeral; was silent for most of the drive home. Finally, he said. "Baby, life's too short to waste it not being happy. Let's do it. You want to move? Let's move."

So we did it. We moved.

By the time I'd finished my Masters, a friend of a friend of my academic advisor told me about a job. It wasn't perfect, no job is, but it looked pretty good, and I would've taken anything that finally got me out of Houston.

Murphy flew out with me for the final interview. He not only got the telecommuting deal from his boss, he also got some time off to move. I wanted to go by myself, but he wouldn't hear of it. He genuinely seemed to believe something terrible would happen to me if I was traveling alone. It was annoying; I'd been traveling alone since I was a teenager.

"You act like I'm going to get kidnapped or something," I told him. "I'm not a child."

"I never said you were," he said. "I still worry about you, though. Anyhow, what's the harm? I can talk to real estate agents while you're interviewing."

Things moved fast after that. I got the job, Murphy found a house, a condo, really, with a layout that was strangely reminiscent of his old duplex back in Montrose. The neighborhood wasn't anything similar, though. Montrose is the hippy/queer/punk part of Houston, or at least it used to be. Our new neighborhood was almost suburban. As far as Murphy was concerned, it was 'the burbs,' but it had rolling green hills, some of which were practically mountains compared to the flatlands of the Texas Gulf Coast.

Closing out Murphy's old duplex turned out to be less of an ordeal than I thought it would be. Whatever secrets or evidence of ghosts I'd expected to find had either vanished when no one was looking or maybe had never really existed in the first place. Not for the first time, I wondered if Murphy was really as strange as I thought or if maybe I was a little nuts.

We sold almost everything; what we didn't sell got packed into a storage container and sent ahead, along with Murphy's old Porsche. The cats came with us, flying first class in valium-induced nirvana in soft-sided carriers crammed under our seats.

"So...is it everything you thought it would be?" We were sitting on the deck of our new/old condo. Murphy had started a fire in the fire pit, but I was still a little cold. I took the wine glass Murphy offered me and pulled an old comforter closer around my shoulders.

"Too soon to tell," I told him. "But it's different."

It was. To anyone who'd grown up on the Gulf Coast, the Pacific Northwest looked like another planet. The sky was bluer, the air was cleaner, and the green of the plants surrounding us was greener. Over the trees, I could see the surrounding hills. Beyond them, I could see mountains.

"Yup, true that. Are you happy?"

I knew that "too soon to tell" wasn't the answer he'd want, even if it were the truth. The real truth was that I didn't know if I was happy or not, and I never had. I had been with Murphy longer than I'd ever been with anyone. When I'd told him I wanted to move, I halfway expected we'd break up first; almost wanted it to happen.

I didn't know if I was happy or not, but I wasn't unhappy. And he loved me.

God help us both. He really, really loved me.

eight: murgenstaern

I know of precisely one way of traversing interstellar or intergalactic space: Under my own power, one light year at a time, before an expanding universe clipped my wings. As far as I know, the ancient and more recent astronauts that have complicated Earth's history are all, with my sole exception, from adjacent parallel universes. It remains an interesting question whether these universes trace back to the same Creator as this one or if there are also parallels to God, but none of that particularly matters to me. My one concern is reuniting with the Creator God that made me and whatever of my siblings remain from Creation's dawn.

The creatures variously described in Earth's folklore as 'moon men,' 'little green men from Mars,' and (more accurately) 'Greys' were, of course, from no such places. They had arrived from Elsewhere, bringing with them technology far in advance of anyone else's, bringing with them as well a client species. The creatures of the same folklore are named as 'sasquatch,' 'yeti,' or 'Bigfoot.'

I found profoundly disturbing the idea that Greys had set one of their lackeys to watch over my home. Precautions I'd taken after my attempted abduction centuries before ought to have made that impossible. The timing bothered me even more. If this were not mere coincidence, it would mean they had known of the Seraphim Stone's arrival in the solar system before even I had known. This would make them even more advanced than previously supposed. It might also confirm a long-standing suspicion of mine that placed them behind that botched abduction.

Too many things were happening at once that should not be happening at all. I was beginning to wonder if I had grown complacent over the years, perhaps a little too sure of my own invulnerability and superiority to the lesser creatures that either evolved on or migrated to this planet. Now that my opportunity to leave this place was at hand, could I have jeopardized it out of sheer arrogance?

I could sense the Seraphim Stone growing closer; I suspected Murphy's guesses at its destination were entirely accurate. When it arrived, I intended to be there.

Leaving the sasquatch chained to the floor, I bid Murphy to follow me up a short staircase to another section of my home, a gallery cut into the side of the ravine he'd plunged into the night before, affording a view of the valley below. He seemed not only recovered from the experience, but different in other ways as well.

"Our friend below has good hearing," I said. "But not so good as to hear this conversation."

"Agreed."

"I no longer have the luxury of awaiting your decision. Are you with me or not?"

"I'm in. I still need to figure out how to keep all of this off Colvin Case's radar, but I'll do it."

"If I may ask, what decided you?"

"You asked me a very goddam good question last night that I just happen to have been asking myself for months. I don't exactly know what I want to do with the rest of my life, but I'm pretty sure that I don't want to spend it dying a little bit at a time from regret and remorse. I've been doing that for most of the last year. It sucks."

"Dying *a little bit at a time* may well be the least of your concerns past this point," I told him.

He shrugged and laughed, still bitter, not quite as nasty. "Yeah, there's always that. When I went through that guardrail last night, I had every reason to believe I'd done screwed the pooch already. It wasn't how I wanted to go out. Now that I've seen some of what you can do, I'm inclined to think this might actually work. Any other tricks up your sleeve I should know about?"

"All shall be revealed by the time it matters."

"Fine, whatever, I'm good with what I've got so far. What's next?"

"What's next is that I am going to return our friend downstairs to the nearest of his people while you make whatever arrangements need to be made to provide cover for your absence. That absence will either not exceed two day's time or very probably be permanent. I should be back in not more than three to four hours. Be prepared to leave."

"Next stop, Area Fifty Whatever, I take it?"

"I think so," I said. "Things are moving fast. So must we."

"Cool. Can you give me a lift?"

"I can do better than that."

Any remaining doubts I may've had about Murgenstaern's fine-control telekinesis went away sometime between watching him fix the damage to my old Porsche by looking at it... and when I got home and had a good look at my modem.

Any remaining doubts about his ability in the heavy lifting TK department went away when the Porsche, myself, and the 'squatch levitated back up to the road surface, more or less to where I'd been before the 'squatch shot my tire out. Any doubts about any other abilities went away when he slung a half-ton of hogtied sasquatch over his shoulder, waved, and sprinted up an old logging road like Steve Austin at what looked like somewhere around 30 MPH and accelerating.

I headed the other way on the same road, which ran into the road I had been trying to take home the night before. As promised, I found my car parked just short of the intersection, the keys still in the ignition. Ten minutes later, I was home.

Whatever Murgenstaern had done to my home security system to get in, he'd been obliging enough to undo it when he left. There was no indication whatever that anyone had gotten past it at all. As for my booby-trapped VPN/modem setup, whatever he had done was basically beyond me. The explosive charge had been removed, it was sitting on my kitchen table, which I found a little unnerving, but the sensors that were supposed to detect any tampering and set off an alarm back in DC were completely convinced they were part of a fully functional bomb. I'd have some explaining to do the next time my home office setup was due for a field inspection, but I had more immediate concerns.

A quick scan through my emails revealed nothing of huge importance. A performance review meeting I hadn't particularly been looking forward to had been moved up from a couple of months out to next week. There were a couple of pissy emails from Case, reiterating suggestions from earlier in my divorce that I should consider either therapy or AA. The really good news was that my team had performed flawlessly in my absence for a change. Our part of the Archangel Array cover-up had worked perfectly. Other emails confirmed Murgenstaern's insider info that the Array itself would shortly be arriving at Area Fifty Whatever.

Responding to Case's emails in a way that meant I might have a job when this was all over took some time and thought, but I eventually realized I didn't really care and just hit 'send.' The neighbors who have my spare key/front-door security code and a fondness for cats were next to make sure the fuzzy little bastards didn't starve if I didn't make it back.

I almost sent an email to Caroline's last known good email address, but I couldn't think of anything to say that I hadn't said already back when she would still write me back. I could tell her that the idea of dying without ever seeing her again was the most lost and lonely feeling I'd ever had, but there wasn't much reason to believe it would matter.

I rummaged around in the trunk containing my old field gear and found a few things that still worked that might come in handy. When I'd done everything else I could do except have a drink I didn't really need, I said goodbye to the kitties, jumped in the old Porsche, and headed off to whatever the hell I was heading off to.

ten: murgenstaern

There was a highway not far from my mountain, a diner on the highway not far from Murphy's home. It was there I had asked him to meet me.

I found him there in a back booth, drinking black coffee and staring at nothing in particular from under the bill of a nondescript black baseball cap. "I guess the 'squatch got all taken care of?" he said as I sat.

"Most certainly," I said, sitting in the opposite side of the booth. "I don't think he will be slipping into town again anytime soon."

"That probably makes two of us."

"You can still stand down from this."

"No, I can't. So, what's next?"

"Just to confirm. The facility you describe as 'Area Fifty Whatever' is a location you can find?"

"Yup. I checked while I was logged into The Company network. They haven't moved it. Still Northern Nevada. It's not the easiest place in the world to get into, but this..." He pulled a plastic ID badge from his pocket. "This gets me in."

"What gets me in?" I asked.

He rummaged in his pocket and produced a second item. "Guest badge. I'm not supposed to have these, but they do come in handy."

"Do you have a full tank of gas?"

"That too."

"Then let's go."

Murphy laughed. "Unless you have another trick or two up your sleeve, it's still a twelve-hour drive."

"Show me the route." Murphy pulled a computer tablet from his bag, handing it to me. I made a couple of adjustments and handed it back.

"That's more like sixteen hours, and that last stretch ain't exactly a road."

"As you say... I have a trick or two."

* * *

I waited until we were east of the Cascades and the sun was low in the sky. "Is this a fast car?" I asked.

"It's old, but it's still a Porsche, dude. It's as fast as you want it to be."

"In that case, please drive as fast as you possibly can."

"It's as fast as you want it to be on a good road. This ain't a good road."

"Trust me on this. And please take no offense if I am slow to answer further questions. This takes a fair amount of my attention."

As he increased his speed, I focused my attention on three things: The car's engine, its contact with the road, and the road ahead to ensure nothing obstructed our way. After a while, Murphy realized what I was doing and sped up even more.

Then more.

The forests gave way to fields that soon became desert, the night sky clear and stark above us. Even with my attention and my powers engaged; part of my mind could still be spared to seek the Seraphim Stone. Through the night sky in my mind's eye, a piece of heaven's fire burned on the horizon before us. Not close, but within my grasp. I willed the Porsche to go a little faster. I was going home.

eleven: murphy

I was headed south toward Nevada in the old Porsche, with Lucifer Morningstar riding shotgun. I was already going too fast on the back roads he'd insisted on taking when he told me to speed up, but I did it anyway. The ride started getting smoother, and the sound of the engine mellowed. On a whim, I sped up. The ride got even smoother. So, of course, I sped up even more.

At one point, I looked at the speedometer. That was a bad idea. Either what he was doing to the engine was causing it to read wrong or the old Porsche was well on its way to the current land speed record, not useful information in either case. I just focused on driving and Murgenstaern focused on whatever the hell it was he was doing. In no time at all, we were in the high desert, rocketing down barren and empty roads.

A kind of highway hypnosis took hold, an odd state of detachment. Part of me began to wonder if any of it was real. Any of it.

I thought over my life, every moment since childhood, and began to wonder just how real any of it was. The Order, The Company, the fallen angel seated next to me. To anyone who had not lived my life, quite a bit of it would sound like fever dreams or extravagant fantasies. My secrets had driven my wife away, but what if they weren't secrets? What if she had simply done what any other sane person would do, finding themselves married to a delusional psychotic? Was I even here now? I thought I was in an old Porsche with the speedometer pegged out on a barely paved desert road. Maybe that was a delusion as well.

And what was I supposed to do when I got to this place I was supposedly going? Bluff my way into a top-secret facility so a fallen angel could retrieve a piece of the firmament and fly home? None of it made sense, none of it. The only real question was whether the psychotic break had occurred before or after Caroline had left me.

But what if Caroline was a delusion as well?

I remembered loving with all my heart and soul someone who, at least for a while, actually loved me back. But what if that fond and bittersweet memory of love was simply the biggest delusion of all? No love, no real life, no purpose, just a road to nowhere, haunted by my own delusions and pain.

As I continued south across the desert and the eastern sky began to lighten, I realized what I had come here to do, what my real plan was.

Of course. It was so simple.

I began to slow to make sure I would not miss the turn. The figure in the seat next to me said nothing. It was, in fact, as motionless as stone.

And perhaps not even real.

I recognized the turn just in time and took it. The road I was on now was steep, with many switchbacks. As I climbed, the eastern sky grew steadily lighter.

Finally, the switchbacks gave way to a short straight stretch pointing up a gradual slope ending in a cliff. Yes, this was why I was here.

I gunned the engine and took my foot off the brake. The car leaped forward into the abyss.

Part 4: Disorder

They say it takes a couple of years to figure out whether or not you like the Pacific Northwest. As many times as Murphy and I had been there, I didn't expect it to take that long, and I was right.

Within a few months, I knew that I hated it.

It was everything. It was nothing. Or maybe a whole lot of nothings. I'd told Murphy I sucked; he didn't believe me. OK, I guess he does now.

My job was everything it was supposed to be. My co-workers were all awesome, nice people.

But they weren't my friends.

Shannon had warned me about it, but she lived in rural Alaska and had picked up the local attitude toward the big cities in Washington and Oregon. It had never been easy for me to make friends; now, it seemed close to impossible. I felt awkward, felt like I didn't fit in.

One time, I heard a recording of myself in a meeting. I was so embarrassed I thought I'd die. I'm not a native Texan like Murphy, but I lived in Houston since I was a kid. I didn't think I had a Texas accent. I was wrong.

It was other things as well. The people I worked with were nice enough, but most of them were younger than me, had never lived anywhere else, and had figured out their careers a long time ago. They were also a pack of pretentious little tattooed hipsters. I never once thought of myself as 'conservative.' After all, I lived in Montrose. Only I didn't live there

89

anymore, and I'd picked up more of the Houston-at-large attitude than I'd ever realized.

And dear god, the weather. The rain wasn't a big deal; the lack of sun was. Murphy and I had always joked about having 'Summer Seasonal Affective Disorder' back in Houston when days on end of triple-digit temperature and humidity meant not going anywhere that wasn't air-conditioned. Real 'Seasonal Affective Disorder' hit me... hard. I began to realize what it meant not to see the sun for weeks on end.

And then there was Murphy.

He hated being called a 'transplant' and worked on acclimating to the Northwest the same way he'd once asked me to help him be 'normal.' Only this time, I couldn't help him. Not that he needed it. For a native Texan, he had even less of an accent than I did and had turned it on and off for years. He stopped saying "y'all" the day we arrived; picked up on "you guys" without missing a beat.

In the same way, he'd once traded silk shirts for button-down oxfords, he traded out the oxfords for flannels and went back to wearing jeans. The day we went to the DMV and got rid of our Texas drivers' licenses, we stopped off at REI and got rain jackets. "That makes it official," Murphy had said. "We are now part of the club."

Only I wasn't even sure I wanted to be a part of the club.

The one thing I had hoped would change for the better actually got worse. Murphy still had secrets. His home office in our new house was more open and accessible than his old one. But in no time at all, it seemed just as cold and strange. The cats stopped going in there for whatever reasons of their own. I stopped going in for mine. The same way no one had ever been invited up to his office in Houston, no one was really welcome to know what he was working on now.

I thought about all the rumors I'd heard over the years. He'd always described what he did as 'confidential.' I joked with him about it, or at least I thought I was joking.

"There's not a single person from your office anywhere within a thousand miles," I said. "Can I ask you how your day went, or is that still a secret?"

"Baby, there's nothing I can tell you that you don't already know. The stuff I work on is… confidential. What differences does it make? I didn't take one penny in pay cut, and now we get to live here."

Of course, he loved it. Loved everything about it. Drove around in the rain with the top down and turned into a total beer snob. He'd already been a coffee snob before we left, got worse. The rampant Northwest hipsterism bothered him not at all after spending almost his entire life in one of the most hipster neighborhoods in the world. "This whole damned city is Montrose with better weather, decent beer, and legal pot. What's not to like?" he'd said.

"The weather," I replied. "A little sun would be nice."

He shrugged. "I had enough sun back in Texas to last several lifetimes. If I never see a thermometer hit a hundred again in my life, I'm okay with that."

We were sitting under an umbrella on a deck behind a pub near my office. Murphy had picked me up after work. As usual, he wanted to stop for a drink on the way home. The one thing he didn't like about being a telecommuter was being home all day. We had the deck to ourselves. None of the locals were going to venture out unless the sun was out. The waitress had given us a dirty look for sitting outside, which Murphy had ignored.

I didn't want to have this conversation in public. I didn't want to have it at all. "I don't know if I'm good with it or not."

"What do you mean?" It was that same puzzled/hurt look he had any time he thought I was unhappy. I used to think it meant he loved me. Now, I just thought it was annoying.

"I'm not sure I want to stay here, Murphy. You ever think about moving again?"

He heaved a long sigh. "No, but I guess I need to now. Tell me about it."

"I don't like my job."

"You never like your job. Not ever, not once."

"I don't really like the climate, and I'm tired of hipsters. I can find another job, and you can take yours with you."

"What about the house we basically put our entire savings into?"

"We could sell it; we could rent it. We have options."

He looked pained, hurt and confused. I felt like I was talking to a child. Was it time to tell him what I really felt?

I couldn't yet, but it was getting harder not to.

When I first met Murphy, the fact that he was older than me didn't matter. "I like older men," I'd told him, and it was true. But I had no idea how old he really was. He looked maybe ten years older than me. Good genes, or maybe something more; it was more like twenty.

He still didn't really look that old, but he was acting old. He wanted to settle down. Being with him was as settled as I'd ever wanted to be...and now I wasn't even sure I wanted that.

He didn't say anything until after the waitress had come and gone with another round.

"I'm not going to lie: I do like it here. It felt like coming home to the home I never knew I had when we moved here." He looked down into his beer and shook his head sadly. "I left behind everything and everyone else I ever knew or loved to come here and make a home with you. I did it because you're the one I can't say 'goodbye' to.

"Come up with a plan, Caroline. Figure out a place you'd rather be. I reckon I got a move or two left in me."

This was the part I really didn't want to talk about. "What if it takes more than 'a move or two'?"

"I don't know, baby. This isn't a perfect place; there aren't any, but it ain't bad, either. And I used to think you loved it here... which might've even been why I fell in love with it, too. I do sometimes wonder if you're ever going to find what you're looking for, or if you'd even know it if you saw it.

"I just know one thing. Every time I wake up and see you, I know I found what I was looking for. There was a Caroline-sized hole in my life I didn't even know was there... until you showed up and filled it." He took a long drag on his beer, looking into the rain at nothing in particular. "We'll figure out something."

It wasn't until the old Porsche was suspended in thin air hundreds of feet from anything else in particular that it occurred to me that what I was doing might qualify in some circles as suicidally crazy.

By which time it was a little late.

As the old car sailed out into the void, I remembered that someone or something was supposed to intervene right about now, but I didn't remember much about the details.

Then, something did intervene.

When the disc-shaped craft materialized over us. My first thought was that it was just another hallucination. Then, an opening irised out in its lower portion, and moonbeams reached for us, strangely visible in the early dawn light.

The moonbeams drew us in. This was beginning to seem very familiar.

By the time the hatch irised shut and my old Porsche had come to rest on it, things were beginning to piece together in my mind. I looked at the person in the seat next to me. No longer a statue, Murgenstaern returned my gaze with a wry smile.

"Not quite as planned," he said. "But interesting."

Jocephus bounded down from a hatch that had opened above us and took station next to the Porsche. Moments later, a familiar figure drifted down thru the same hatch.

Evangeia had traded the boardroom attire of our last encounter for beatnik classic black leggings and turtleneck, drawn her coppery hair into a braid that revealed the gracefully pointed ears. Barefoot, as usual. She was floating through the air in full lotus, came to rest on the hood of the

Porsche, and unfolded her long legs, looking vaguely like a car commercial model. Except for the ears, of course.

"You may not realize this," she said. "But you have been under psychic attack for most of the last hundred miles. So have you," she said, nodding toward Murgenstaern. "Which I had not thought possible."

"Your adversaries have acquired some interesting new abilities, Evangeia," Murgenstaern said. "Good to see you, of course. It has been what? 800 years?"

"On that order," she replied.

"You guys know each other?" I asked.

"Somewhat," Murgenstaern said. "I did not found your Order, but you are hardly my only acquaintance within it."

"Well, that's good to know, now."

"I have a reasonable idea of what you were attempting to do and even a vague suspicion as to why," Evangeia said. "Under ordinary circumstances, it might've even worked. These are not ordinary circumstances."

No kidding, I thought.

As her ice-blue eyes settled fully upon me, I once again had the feeling a mouse has when it realizes it's about to be the main course on someone's menu. "You should not have withheld from me your dealings with this... person, but it is understandable that you did. Describing him as persuasive is something of an understatement. It is somewhat a given as well that you have been under a certain amount of personal stress.

"Any lapses in your behavior as a member of this Order to date are a matter I am prepared to overlook, but no more. And while I appreciate the delicacy of your situation as a double agent, I must insist that you remember that your primary loyalty is to us, not The Company. We will do everything possible to preserve your cover, but it is far from our highest current priority."

She turned to Murgenstaern. "As for you, this is hardly the first time you have suborned our people or endangered those I am sworn to protect. I am sure you feel you have good reason for all this—you always do—but you know better than anyone which particular path is paved with good intentions.

"I can no more truly compel you than could any mortal, nor do I wish you any particular harm. But you may find yourself in true need of allies, not entertainment, for the first time in a very long time... perhaps ever."

Kids always hate it when mom and dad fight, but it can also be hella fun. In the three days I had known Murgenstaern, I had not seen him particularly deterred or visibly impressed by much of anything, but if he had anything to say right now, he was keeping it to himself. In the twenty-plus years I had known Evangeia, she had largely seemed even less human to me than Murgenstaern in statue mode and about as impassioned. This was something new.

It occurred to me that they were probably speaking English for my benefit. Eight hundred years? It could have as easily been some obscure dialect of Old Occitan if not ancient Sumerian.

"At the very least, you are going to explain to me your business here to my satisfaction," Evangeia continued. "You may find me more agreeable with your intentions than you think, but you will not interfere with mine."

Murgenstaern spoke. "I have no commitment to your Order, have other commitments predating the existence of Murphy's species, your species, and your respective single-celled ancestors. It would be best if we compare our respective intentions. You first." As usual, it was not a request.

"By all means," Evangeia replied. "Murphy needs to know, and so do you.

"The Black Rock Advanced Research and Containment Facility is operated by a consortium of interests within the U.S. military and intelligence communities. The Order both monitors this facility and maintains deep-cover brethren within its staff.

"Shortly after the arrival of the downed surveillance device called 'The Archangel Array,' we became aware that this facility was being subjected to extremely low-frequency electromagnetic energy with fairly unusual characteristics. Some hours later, all contact with the facility was lost, including contact with The Order's own deep-cover assets.

"I was dispatched to investigate. Upon arrival, I determined that a beam of the same unusual low-frequency energy was apparently tracking a ground object in the desert north of here, which turned out to be a vintage Porsche convertible moving toward this location at ballistic speeds.

"We have determined that Black Rock is currently under attack. Under the terms of Protocol 23, I am taking command of this facility. Any questions regarding the disposition of any materials presently housed here shall be addressed to me. In fact, any questions regarding anything whatever more recent than the early formation of the universe should be going to me.

"Am I clear?"

Although I am with few peers in what Murphy might describe as 'multitasking,' even I have limits.

Between keeping Murphy's antique vehicle intact and in place at extreme velocity on what could be charitably described as a 'road,' batting away the occasional coyote or rabbit before they wound up on the front of the car, and making sure that the Seraphim Stone remained our destination, I was handling a number of things at once, requiring a fair degree of attention. Other than making sure he was still conscious, I had little attention to spare for Murphy. I didn't expect him, in any case, to make small talk over the hurricane-force slipstream I was guiding past our heads with my mind. Possibly, I might have noticed other small changes taking place in him under better circumstances. Or perhaps not. Again, I am not a mind reader.

But under almost any other circumstances, I would have noticed that I had lost the ability to move.

What Murphy describes as my 'statue mode' is simply what happens when I'm busy doing something else and have the luxury of not animating the puppet that enables me to pass as human. By the time we were approaching the location of 'Area Fifty Whatever,' I had been immobile for many hours.

Driving off a cliff had actually been part of our plan, although not a part Murphy had agreed to without considerable persuasion. "You drove off a cliff yesterday," I'd said. "I fail to see the difference." We had been sitting in the diner going over the final details. For the sake of appearances, I had ordered coffee as well.

Murphy glared at me. "The difference is that I was drunk, and a fucking sasquatch had shot out my tire. This time, I'm cold-sober and doing it on purpose. They're also a few hundred odd feet more elevation involved."

"A few thousand more feet would not make a difference. And I will be sitting in the car as well."

"Big deal. If there's some sort of 'oopsie,' you still get to walk away from the crash."

"More likely crawl, but I take your point."

"I'm not sure I take yours. This little 'shortcut' of yours isn't going to get us past any security checkpoints that matter or shave off any trip time that couldn't be shaved off by taking a more direct route."

"No, but the entire route keeps us clear of several excellent spots for an ambush. You and I have both been under surveillance for a week. Are you so very sure the roads will not be watched?"

He had eventually agreed, as I knew he would. In the overall scope of what we were doing, driving off a cliff in the company of a telekinetically gifted elder being was the least of his worries.

But even so, I found myself surprised when he turned on to the cutoff to the mesa without a single word of protest or wisecrack. I thought to comment on this.

And was even more surprised to find I could not do so.

Someone or something had found a way to interfere with my ability to control my puppet. Whatever they were doing was beyond subtle; I had sensed nothing.

There was never any real danger of a crash only one of us was going to crawl away from. I could probably even move my puppet's limbs through

99

sheer force of my abilities, but I would certainly break it in the process, and certainly, I could not speak. I'm fond of my puppet; I've put a lot of work into it. Despite my plans to abandon it altogether, I hated the idea of breaking it any more than I had to.

As Murphy unhesitatingly drove off the cliff, I began the process of lowering the car to the road below my 'shortcut' and considered my various options.

I was still considering when a craft of The Order appeared and took us aboard. As soon as we were within its walls, I found I could move again. I also realized that whatever had happened involved more than a mere shutdown of my puppet. Somehow, during the drive from the Northwest, my senses had been subtly limited in a way I had never experienced and had not noticed. Now restored, I was fairly sure I knew how it had been done and by whom.

"Not quite as planned," I'd said to Murphy, "but interesting."

Evangeia de Lourdes' subsequence appearance was not entirely surprising, her claims of authority even less so.

All the extradimensionals that have taken varying levels of residency on Earth are to some degree related to humankind, representing either what humans became in other realities or what wound up taking their place. Some of them are as closely related as were once humans and Neanderthals, with predictably similar results.

Evangeia was one such result. We'd met before, back when I was only slightly masquerading as human, and she was doing her best to masquerade as a god. She'd been willful and arrogant back then as well and almost got burned at the stake for it. I hadn't exactly expected to be thanked for my troubles then, expected it less now, but I did have something of what Murphy might call 'a marker,' and I had every intention of calling it in.

"...in fact, any questions regarding anything whatever more recent than the early formation of the universe should be going to me. Am I clear?"

"Abundantly," I said. "One small question, though, if I may."

"By all means."

"Should it be the case that material presently housed in this facility includes items dating back to 'the early formation of the universe,' are you willing to take into account subject matter expertise in how best to deal with such items?"

Evangeia raised one brow. "If the subject matter expert in question is yourself, I'll take it under advisement, perhaps as soon as you explain what exactly it is you want and what you are doing here. Keep it simple, Morningstar, and try not to condescend too much to us mere mortals."

"I can make it very simple. How would you like me gone from this place?"

"I expect you gone from this facility in any event, although Murphy will not be leaving with you."

"That's not what I mean. How would you and your Order like me gone from this planet?"

"I have no opinion on your residency one way or another. The Grandmasters have long seen you as a threat, but many think you may have diminished to the point of merely being an unpredictable nuisance. Is this planet better off without you? Probably.

"In any case, it was my understanding you were stuck here, absent the possibility of humanity leaving this place and offering you a ride. Is this not so?"

"No longer. I can go home, Evangeia. My means to do so is on your base yonder that you claim under attack."

"What struck the Archangel Array out of orbit is no spaceship, certainly not one big enough to hold you."

"I don't need a spaceship. What struck down that artifact is as much a remnant of creation's dawn as I am. I call it the Seraphim Stone, and it calls to me. With it, it is finally within my power to leave this place."

"Or rule it."

"And when was that ever my intent? Milton was wrong, and the words he put in my mouth were utterly foolish. Far better to serve in Heaven. I was never cast out, you know, nor truly fallen. All I really want is to go home… and again do the bidding of my Master."

"I need more."

"You described what is happening to your facility as an 'attack.' I agree with that description. Although you've not named the attackers, I think we agree as well who they are."

"The Selenites," Evangeia said, setting her mouth in a grim line of distaste.

"Yes," I said. "I believe they want the same thing I want… but for different reasons.

"Some time ago, unknowns in human guise attempted to abduct me from this universe. I now believe they were in the employ of your Selenites." I turned to Murphy. "Greys, I think they are now called."

He shrugged. "I've heard them called lots of things."

I turned back to Evangeia. "The attempt failed. I made sure it failed on such a scale that a repeated effort would be unlikely."

"Why the attempt in the first place?"

I had wondered that myself on many occasions. Not everything that slipped through the cracks in the universe was sentient or even dangerous, but the Greys were both. Evangeia's people and a few others had learned to navigate the cracks in space. The Greys apparently created them at will. They were far from omnipotent, however, and a delicate balance of power had existed between them and the other visitor races almost since the cracks first opened.

The Greys' interest in proto-matter from the beginning of time could be utterly benign and academic.

Or not.

"What I am as a being, an entity, I doubt is of any more importance to them than any other creature they abduct or mutilate for whatever reason. But I am, at my core, a uniquely powerful remnant from the early creation of this universe. Call it Dawn Matter if you like, but there is nothing else in this or any other universe remotely like it. I am not 'star stuff'. I'm the stuff that existed before the stars and galaxies I helped to create... so is the Seraphim Stone.

"I have no idea what your Selenites want with such stuff, no interest in finding out. Some transcendentally powerful tool or weapon? Probably. It doesn't seem likely to be anything in your best interest in any case. If I depart and take the Seraphim Stone with me, the balance of power and everything else here remains exactly the same, with the exception of my absence. Problem solved, I would say."

"Will they not attempt your pursuit?"

I mimicked Murphy's shrug. "They are welcome to try, but they are no more capable of true interstellar travel than you are. And if they persist in the matter, I'm happy to remind them of the last time they took too much interest in my affairs."

"And your word on this, you will simply take this power object and leave?"

"My word."

"I must confer with my masters on this, but I will. The sworn word of Lucifer Morningstar is sufficient to me," Evangeia said.

She came closer and touched my puppet's face. "I do not forget," she said.

The marker had called in itself.

four: murphy

I should not have been surprised when Murgenstaern talked Evangeia into it. After all, the persuasive bastard had talked me into driving off a cliff, but the ease with which he had pulled it off was nonetheless impressive. Whatever had happened 800 years ago between them likely made for one damned interesting field report in The Order's archives I will never get to read.

Which suits me just fine.

Things started happening rapidly after that. Protocol 23 had only been invoked a few times before. It meant that The Order was intervening directly to deal with something the Grandmasters consider a planetary-level emergency. The Grandmasters take the long view, and their definition of an 'emergency' is guaranteed to make the hairs stand up on the back of your neck.

Luckily, baseline humans who haven't made bad life decisions about meddling in the affairs of wizards and aliens either don't get to hear about these things or hear a carefully sanitized version when something like this does happen. To a certain degree, my roles within The Company and The Order mirror each other and even involve some of the same tools. The main difference is scope: The Company hardly ever asks me to rewrite history. The Order seldom asks for much less.

The aftermath of Protocol 23 actions have involved huge rewrites and frequently as well involve the Greys, or 'Selenites,' as the older Grandmasters call them. At least part of the reason Evangeia had been an easy sell for Murgenstaern's pitch was the involvement of those little termite rat bastards. They were a big part of the reason The Order even existed in the first place. We had been containing their activity on Earth for the better part of five hundred years. Almost every other species that had come in through the cracks in space had had a problem with the Greys at one time or another, in some cases, long before coming to Earth.

Whatever they wanted with the Seraphim Stone, whatever they'd wanted when they attempted their silly damned abduction trick on Murgenstaern, no one believed it was going to benefit anyone else, and no one found it particularly difficult to believe that the end result would not wind up a weapon pointed at their mutual heads or head equivalents.

And while the Seraphim Stone was precisely the sort of artifact The Order would love to have in its archives, keeping it could be a problem. The Greys would keep trying to get their hands on it; eventually, they'd succeed. The Stone had no real use in this universe except as a bargaining chip... or a fallen angel's ticket home.

I didn't get to sit in on the call, but Evangeia didn't get to make a decision like this on her own. Even though I don't report up in The Order past her, I've met some of the greater Masters on occasion. Regardless of their actual DNA, I wouldn't exactly describe any of them as 'human,' and I think that might've played a role in the decision as well.

All I really knew of the being that called itself 'Lucifer Morningstar' was what that being had told me and abilities I'd witnessed that gave good reason to believe the claims were true. But there was something more. I'm no psychic, and Murgenstaern claimed that the content of human minds were as opaque to him as a stone wall would be to me. But you would have to be made of stone to not sense the loneliness emanating from him like waves of cold.

Evangeia and those like her are psychic, or at least say they are, and they live lives spanning thousands of years. Almost as much a brief nothing as my own life to a thing that had essentially lived for all of time, but long enough to know what it's like to watch entire civilizations turn to dust, entire species vanish. Long enough to imagine what it must be like to watch it again and again and again... without even the company of other immortals.

I think Murgenstaern was right that the Grandmasters would be happy to see him gone, but I think compassion figured into the decision as well. Even a lowly human like me could tell that all the poor bastard wanted was to go home. For whatever reason... everyone with a say in the matter agreed it was a good idea. Now he just had to go get his ticket.

And that was about to get complicated. Area Fifty Whatever was already under attack. Just not physically. Not yet, anyway.

* * *

"We've no way of knowing how any one individual might react," Evangeia said. "Extreme paranoia is not unlikely, nor suicidal ideation. Delusions are certainly possible, perhaps even hallucinations."

"Or, in my case, deciding your whole damned life is a hallucination," I said.

If my life really was a hallucination, the really good drugs had finally kicked in. I was sitting in a conference room with Murgenstaern and Evangeia. The assault team commander that would assist in re-taking Area Fifty Whatever was also at the table, with a couple of his aides.

The Order is not, never has been, a military organization. The original human Grandmasters had been an alchemist and a spy. There had been no shortage of mercenaries available as needed in Elizabethan England; there were plenty now. In some ways, the available talent was better than ever. The assault team commander and his boys were some of the best talent money could buy.

I pitied the human foolish enough to get in their way.

The assault team were members of another Elsewhere species. They were tight-lipped about their intentions on Earth but party to the same detente as The Order's nonhuman patrons.

Actually, they were just tight-lipped in general.

Roughly humanoid, at least to the point of being able to wear off-the-rack tactical gear (except for the boots), their species had made their way from a universe where a significant asteroid strike had failed to occur sixty-odd million years ago.

Despite being called 'reptilian' in popular paranormal paperbacks, they are at least as warm-blooded as my associates in The Company (which isn't saying that much, of course).

The assault team commander's eyes would've been perfectly at home in a crocodile's skull, and even though his own skull could have passed for human, the jaws and teeth plainly belonged to a carnivore. I couldn't pronounce and won't even try to spell his name. Let's just call him Commander Hiss.

"All humansss are paranoid," he said. "And any that sssee my team will think they are hallucccinating asss well."

"That's why your team will be wearing balaclavas for the duration of this exercise," Evangeia said. "I'd like to keep the clean-up on this as light as possible."

The entirety of Black Rock was under the same form of psychic attack that had slipped me off the rails driving across the desert. We knew the Greys could control human minds under certain conditions, but they had never attempted to control as many people at once as would be needed to simply seize the facility and take the Seraphim Stone. Driving everyone on the base slightly bonkers from orbit was another matter. They'd done things like this before. My previous plan to bluff my way into the Black Rock Advanced Research and Containment Facility was null and void. The entire facility was now on lockdown. It would take more than my credentials to get in.

I knew the layout, though, and could direct Hiss and his team to a good spot to break in. There wasn't going to be anything subtle about this. There wasn't time. A simple smash-and-grab operation I would be spinning disinformation about for the rest of my career, assuming I had one. Hiss and his team would get us in. Murgenstaern and I would make our way to the Seraphim Stone. We didn't need to know exactly where it was being kept. His senses would lead us straight to it.

After that, the plan got a little vague. Murgenstaern had given his word he would be 'gone' the moment The Stone was in his possession. Hiss and his team would mop up any unfriendlies that may or may not have arrived, and The Order would spirit me away to start writing press releases about how an entire research facility had gotten high on contaminated rye bread from the commissary. Or something. I'd figure it out.

Under their balaclavas, Hiss and his team would be wearing what might as well be called tinfoil hats. That's what they looked like, and they served exactly the same purpose of preventing alien mind control. I'd be wearing one as well, but not Murgenstaern. He had been attacked by something different, something he believed he could prevent being used again. He did not elaborate on the details.

Whatever else Commander Hiss might not have liked about this operation, very little pleased him less than Murgenstaern's involvement. "Thiss thing has lied sssince the beginning of time. Trussting it iss folly."

"Neither your decision nor your concern, Commander," Evangeia replied. "Your team has been engaged for the purpose of gaining access to our base and providing ground support until we are ready to leave. Strategic advice exceeds your current paygrade."

"And I intend to keep my word," Murgenstaern interjected. "Do not think for a moment there is a single thing on this world that might keep me here for even a minute once I am finally able to leave, or that there is anything on this world or any other that might prevent me from coming and going as I please and am able."

"The Greysss might not agree."

"What they did was less effective than they thought, will not be repeated, and does not matter, for I am leaving, and where I go, none may follow."

"SSSee that you do," Hiss replied. "And if you do not, think not to hide onccce more among humanssss."

"I'm not even going to ask what you did to piss off the Sauroids," I said.

"Good," Murgenstaern said.

Evangeia's flying saucer hovered over the mountain I'd driven off the day before. Commander Hiss had arrived for the meeting in an equivalent craft of his own, a blunt, iron-gray cylinder parked nearby on stubby landing legs. Hiss's team was in place between them, gearing up for the assault. Under the balaclavas, they passed for human, as long as you didn't take a close look at their booted feet.

We would soon be joining them in their craft for the short hop down to the base. What the Sauroid vehicle lacked in aesthetics, it made up for in functionality. Its stealth capability was equal to any craft of the Order's. We would arrive undetected.

Murgenstaern and I were sitting on a rock outcropping near Evangeia's saucer. No one had said, "Smoke 'em if you got 'em," but I was. I'd offered him one as well out of conditioned politeness. For whatever reasons of his own, he accepted.

Below us, the barren playa stretched out to the horizon. Close to the horizon to the south, we could see the lights and structure of Area Fifty Whatever, including the truly massive structures in the facility's center. The scale was deceptive, even so. Most of 'The Black Rock Advanced Research and Containment Facility' was many levels underneath what had once been a discarded airbase.

I took a drag and exhaled. "There is something I'd like to ask you about."

"You may certainly ask." Murgenstaern seemed oblivious to the assault team, barely aware of me. At a guess, I'd say the Seraphim Stone to which he now had direct line of 'sight,' had most of his attention.

"You invited me along on this ride because I have 'unique subject matter expertise' on both The Company and The Order. You've got some 'unique subject matter expertise' of your own."

"One could say."

"As far as I know, you are the sole living being on this planet that can claim a first-person relationship with God based on anything other than wishful thinking or self-delusion."

"You perhaps judge too harshly."

I laughed. "I don't think so. Every single human who ever claimed to be buddies with The Big Guy has contradicted everyone else, making that claim beyond any credibility. They're either making shit up or having a comfortable delusion, but not you. You're not human, and you were actually there."

"You said you had a question."

"Yeah, I do. Even though the basic design of this universe left you stranded on Earth and opened up holes in space used by little gray bastards that apparently would like to dissect you, you seem to believe that everything that has happened in the several billion years since God made you is according to His plan. Every... single... thing. Do you have a reason to think that... or are you just as deluded as the folks that tried to sell me a bill of goods back in Sunday School?"

I pretty much expected him to blow me off or go into 'statue mode' while thinking about it. To my surprise, he did neither.

"You will probably not like the answer. I've considered this very question for longer than any of your kind could have even asked it. My one reason for believing as I do is no different than those of your kind you consider 'deluded.'" He took a drag on his own cigarette. "Essentially, it is a matter of faith."

"You gotta be shitting me. The one and only Lucifer Morningstar is solely motivated by what amounts to love and faith in God?"

"Essentially, yes."

I stubbed out my cigarette on the rock next to me. "They need to do some serious work on Sunday School curriculum."

"Undoubtedly."

"Then everything does happen for a reason?"

"I did not say that. The universe, as I understand it, is an unfolding fractal. The basic outline of that fractal is present in every single piece of it, down past levels you would understand. But consciousness and free will have been parts of that design since before I existed. I chose exile on this world in obedience to what could be considered 'the will of God,' but it was my choice, Murphy."

"But God made you before even the galaxies themselves. You can't say you weren't made in such a way that choice was inevitable."

The archangel shrugged. "I've considered that possibility as well. If God intended me to choose millions of years of exile in this place, then God is more implacably cruel than anything else in God's universe. But that is not for me to judge." He stubbed out his cigarette as well. "In any event, I look forward to discussing the matter upon my return."

* * *

There was barely room for Murgenstaern and me to squeeze into the hold of the Sauroid assault craft. To one, the hulking mercenaries around us were dressed in the black tactical gear favored by human mercs and the occasional SWAT team (minus body armor they didn't need), with balaclavas, safety goggles that mostly served to conceal their eyes, and mind control deterrent 'tinfoil' tucked up under the balaclavas.

I was more or less dressed the same way, with the exception of my old bike jacket. Murgenstaern was wearing the same leather trench coat he'd mostly been wearing since I'd first met him, over his standard gray suit and dark shirt. No surprise there; he was even less concerned about getting shot than the Sauroids, didn't need a tinfoil hat, and passed as human, at least until you got to know him. If Area Fifty Whatever's security force was still functional, they'd probably just assume he was in charge and shoot him first.

Once everyone was in, the hatch was raised shut, and we were off. I'd already shown Hiss and his pilot where to sit down.

It was a short ride. Minutes later, the hatch dropped again. We'd traveled twenty miles and descended a few hundred feet to the desert floor adjacent to the facility perimeter. There were no alarms or any other sign we'd been detected. Apparently, the Sauroid's tech was as good as they claimed.

The assault team filed out rapidly, taking formation around the place in the fence I'd told them to place the charges while the demolition tech did his work. So far, everything was going to plan.

Then, suddenly, it wasn't.

The Gray mothership filled the sky from nowhere, a black triangle at least a thousand feet across.

The first shot took out the assault craft, which apparently wasn't so stealthy after all. Instead of disappearing into a glowing ball like an old sci-fi movie, it violently blew apart like a more current flick, with plenty of shrapnel.

"Go!" I screamed at the demo tech. I needn't have bothered. He fell back, and the fence blew.

Additional shots started hitting members of the assault team. This time they did vanish like an old sci-fi flick effect, in puffs of dust and smoke.

The demo tech managed to rig the inner wall before getting hit. Luckily, the detonator was intact. Even better luck: It was, like the rest of the Sauroid gear, off-the-shelf. I sprinted to where it had been dropped, dived to one side, and hit the button. The wall blew.

By the time what was left of the assault team had gotten through the hole in the wall, half the team had gone up in puffs of glowing red smoke. Hiss had been taken out with the drop ship.

Whatever the Greys had been using apparently didn't work through concrete. We were safe, but not for long. "Okay," I said. "You guys are working for The fucking Order, and that's me. I need to know who's in command."

There was a long silence. Finally, one of the mercs said, "We ssstill get paid, yessss?"

"Yup."

"Then we follow you."

five: murgenstaern

It had all been conjecture (and the word of a lying sasquatch) to the point that the Selenite craft appeared above us. I had never truly known who

114

had been behind my attempted abduction centuries before. Neither did I know with any certainty than anyone but myself had plans for the Seraphim Stone...it was just not a possibility I could chance.

Once we were in the containment facility, the 'light' of the Stone was brighter to my inner vision than ever. I cannot describe what I felt in human terms. Elation at ending my exile? Certainly. Anxiety that even now, there was a chance this could be taken from me? Very much so. But there were other feelings as well that I cannot describe to mortals, even Evangeia's relatively long-lived kind. And for a moment, those feelings overwhelmed me.

Then, I mastered myself. There was still work to be done.

Murphy had peeled the balaclava away from his face, the better to give orders to those he now commanded. He'd appropriated a sidearm from the Sauroids. Even though the rest of their gear seemed to have been purchased in bulk from Amazon, their weapons had been supplied by The Order. They superficially looked like conventional human firearms. They weren't.

"Okay, here's the drill," Murphy said, holding up his weapon and pointing to the stock. "Nonlethal setting for humans, even humans that happen to be shootin' back. Any non-humans not part of this team will be assumed hostile. Light 'em up as you see fit, but only after I give the word.

"This guy," he nodded at me. "Is on point and taking us to the target. Once a target is acquired, we hold position until the target and our scout have left the building. We will then make our way back the way we came in.

"You," he pointed to the Sauroid who had spoken earlier. "Whatever your rank was before, you are now second in command. If anything happens to me, proceed as planned and get your people out of here. Any questions?"

"Yesssss," said Murphy's newly appointed second. "What keepsss the Greyss from vaporizing us asss ssoon asss we are in the open?"

"Good question." Murphy turned to me. "I'm pretty sure adepts of The Order are monitoring us already, but I hate to ask these guys to depend on that. Do you have a way to contact Evangeia?"

"Not now," I replied. "Once the Seraphim Stone is in my possession, there is very little upon this planet I cannot do."

"In that case, and despite your sworn word to leave immediately, I want your word as well that you will arrange a ride for these guys."

"You have it. What of yourself?"

"Let's assume I'm riding with them."

* * *

As we made our way further into the Black Rock facility, it soon became evident that Murphy's concerns over lethal force being used against any 'humans that happen to be shooting back' were not needed. After over a day of the same type of psychic attack that had left Murphy detached and suicidal after a few hours, the humans we encountered were either catatonic or apparently detached from their surroundings and incapacitated. Some were slumped in chairs in the offices and cubicles we passed. Others curled into fetal balls in the hallways and corridors. Some stared blankly at nothing apparent. Others saw us, either giggling or whimpering as we continued.

"Are they hallucinating?" I asked Murphy.

"I'd say they're tripping their fucking balls off."

Despite Murphy's knowledge of the facility, we still hit a couple of dead ends while making our way to the containment area where the Archangel

Array and the Seraphim Stone were being held. The closer we approached, the clearer the Stone's location was in my mind.

"How close do you need to get?" Murphy asked me.

"This is not a thing I can move with my mind if that is what you mean. I have to go to it. I have to touch it."

"Does that apply to the Greys as well? They can also move things at a distance."

"If they could do such a thing to either the Stone or myself, I would not be here now."

"I guess not."

A few more twists and turns through the corridors, more terrified or catatonic people huddled into corners or laughing or crying. Also bodies. Murphy was not the only one who had been driven to thoughts of suicide.

"I don't want to jinx anything," Murphy said. "But it's looking like we might actually pull this off."

"Indeed."

"It's been real, and it's been fun, old son, and even if I can't exactly say it's been real fun, I can say that I will miss you, Lucifer Morningstar. Milton and my old Sunday School teacher had it all wrong."

"Not all, I fear...but the sentiment is appreciated."

A few more turns, then we rounded one last corner. My inner vision of the Stone and my outer vision of a way forward were one. At the end of the corridor was a massive door that could have functioned well for a bank vault or a nuclear facility. It may or may not have exceeded what I could simply move with my mind, but I felt sure that the inner workings of whatever locked it would be no challenge. I walked toward it, focusing all my senses.

"This ain't right," Murphy said. I ignored him.

"It can't be this easy," he said. "I have a really, really bad feeling about this."

I tuned it out, tuned all of it out. All my attention was focused on the barrier before me and what lay past.

The light from the Seraphim Stone filled my inner vision. I would be free again, finally free of this place. No more talking monkeys, no more talking lizards, no more talk.

As I grew closer, the workings of the door came clear to me. It would be easy.

The thought that I would soon again be truly part of the cosmos was a thing beyond words, almost a thing beyond thought. As I grew closer, the light from the Seraphim Stone sang within me, brighter, brighter...

Only to go out.

six: murphy

I'd only been in Area Fifty Whatever once before, but I didn't exactly need to know it like the back of my hand. Murgenstaern knew where he was going. I just needed to be able to badge us through the occasional security gate and not step on any of the staff who had gone catatonic from psychic bombardment.

As soon as I saw the blast door between ourselves and the Archangel Array / Seraphim Stone, I knew I wasn't going to just badge us in. All our C4 had gone up in a puff of red smoke along with the demolition tech. I had no idea if Murgenstaern's telekinesis was up to the challenge, but I suspected we were about to find out.

Leading an assault team on a raid had brought back a lot I'd forgotten or compartmentalized, including instincts not needed for the bureaucratic infighting of a desk job. And I always listen to my instincts.

There were only two ways out of this place. One involved a soon-to-be omnipotent archangel keeping his word, the other involved leading my team back out the way we came. One involved the aforementioned and not-yet omnipotent archangel getting through several tons of door; the other required nothing more challenging than not stepping on mostly living people who had been mind fucked by aliens.

Only maybe not.

"This ain't right," I said to Murgenstaern, who ignored me.

"It can't be this easy," I said to his receding back. "I have a really, really bad feeling about this."

What was left of the assault team had followed us into the corridor. Bad idea. I was going to order them back out when two things happened, one unexpected, the other supposedly impossible.

A shot rang out, loud, high-caliber. Murgenstaern pitched forward, as apparently dead as anyone else who'd been shot in the back.

I threw myself against the wall, then turned. Colvin Case was at the far end of the corridor, holding a .45 revolver like he actually knew how to use it and apparently just had. Behind him stood a triad of Greys. Behind them, they had an assault team of their own. I never thought even one sasquatch with a rifle was a good idea.

"Did you really think you were the only one?" Case said.

seven: caroline

It wasn't just the age thing.

Murphy had grown up poor, an only child of people who wound up being married to each other for fifty years. My parents weren't rich, but they weren't poor. They stayed married just long enough to make sure I'd be old enough to be traumatized by the custody battles and head games.

Bottom line: When our own marriage got rocky, I had one set of expectations... and Murphy had another.

I stuck it out as long as I could. I did everything I could. But at a certain point, it was obvious to me that it wasn't working. Murphy wouldn't see it, couldn't see it. When I finally had to tell him what I had to do, it might well have been the worst day of his life.

But not mine.

It had become inevitable.

I picked fights with him. I'm not proud of it, but I'm not ashamed, either. He stubbornly, obstinately, refused to admit we had problems.

The fights became more frequent, the makeup sex after the fights started to dwindle away. The occasional drinking turned into constant drinking.

I needed space and he couldn't see it, didn't even understand the concept. He wanted to be married the way his parents had been married.

I didn't want to be married any more at all.

It was everything, or it was nothing. Or maybe a whole lot of nothings.

After two years of struggling with my job, I turned in my resignation. Rather than deal with yet another Pacific Northwest winter, I cashed out my savings and used the airline miles we'd been sitting on for years to plan a trip to all the places we were once going to see that somehow never happened.

I told him I was coming back. But we both knew that wasn't really going to happen.

Neither one of us said a word on the drive to the airport. Typically, he put the top down even though there was occasional light rain drizzling from the gray Northwest skies. Whenever he could take his eyes from the road, he looked at me, but I couldn't look at him.

I just... ouldn't.

Finally, we wound up at the security gate in the airport. He couldn't hug me around my loaded backpack, but he kissed me until I couldn't stand it anymore and made him stop.

Then I turned and walked away.

For one crazy moment, I wanted just to ditch the backpack, turn around, tell him I was sorry, and ask him to take me home. Then, the moment passed. I went on with my life.

I suck, Murphy, I always told you that. Maybe now you'll finally believe me. Maybe now, you'll finally stop loving me.

You really should, you know.

eight: murphy

By Gulf Coast standards, it had been a nice day.

Case had flown in from D.C. It was the first time any of us had seen him since we'd found out he was going to be our boss. I had myself only gotten back into town a few days ago. Caroline and I had gone to see Shannon again and had made a decision.

I hadn't been surprised that Case accepted the invitation to a long off-campus lunch, but I was surprised when he ordered a margarita. That sort of behavior was frowned upon by the current Company management he was trying very hard to blend in with.

We were sitting on the patio at Hugo's in Montrose, not far from my house. The downtown skyline was visible through the muggy, smoggy air, including the building where our 'consulting firm' kept its offices.

"I never had a chance to tell you how sorry I was about your parents." Case had shed his jacket and loosened his tie. I didn't have a tie to loosen, my one jacket was hanging on a peg in my cube back at the office. Lack of rank has its privileges. The big blond kid I used to get into after-hour clubs was getting skinny and sober and working his way up the ladder, but he was still my friend...sort of.

"Thanks," I told him.

"How's Caroline?"

"She's good. She's wrapping up her master's in a few weeks and thinking about a new job."

"Congratulate her for me. How many does that make?"

"Job or degree? I've pretty much lost count either way."

Case chuckled. "Pretty much just the one job in your case, even though you could've had mine."

I shrugged. "You look better in a suit than I do, and swapping Houston for D.C. doesn't strike me as much of an improvement. But there is something I want to talk to you about... and I think you know what it is."

Case sipped his 'rita. The waiter brought us some more chips, as well as some of the fried grasshoppers I'd gotten fond of back when I still did field work.

"Pretty much," Case said. "But I still want to hear it from you."

"After saying goodbye to Mom and Dad for the last time, I realized there wasn't one single thing or person in this world I wouldn't say goodbye to as well, except for one.

"She's not happy here, Colvin. There's not a thing in this world I won't do for her, not a place in this world I won't go for her. There's really just one thing holding me here. And maybe not even that."

"Are we talking about your resignation... or something else?"

"Something else." I took a deep breath. Case was sort of my friend, and now he was my boss. No *sort of* about it. He could shoot the whole thing down in a heartbeat. But I'd taken worse chances for less. "At any given time, I'm having up to half a dozen simultaneous IM conversations with analysts or technicians, including the ones sitting in cubes next to me. Except for policy, there's not a single damn reason I can't do what I do anywhere in the world with a decent Internet connection."

Case took off his glasses and rubbed his eyes briefly. "'Policy' in our case is no small matter. Implementing a telecommute option in an insurance office or a software company is one thing. Implementing it in The Company... is a little more complicated."

"But not impossible."

"Hardly. There's a pilot program back in D.C., which I'm assuming you already know about since we're having this conversation."

"Yup." I couldn't read him. He was either going to say "yes" or "no." That much I knew. I also knew there wouldn't be much point in arguing about it either way.

"What you may not know is that there are a lot of restrictions and requirements, including some technical ones involving equipment I would prefer not to have in my home. Have you talked to Caroline about this?"

"A little. You know I don't tell tales out of school."

"No, you don't, which is one reason this could work. Do you know where you're going?"

"At this point, it looks like probably Portland or Seattle, although there's a few other places as well."

"All in the Northwest, I take it?"

"Yup."

"I'll put in the request, Murphy. You're a valuable asset I would prefer we keep. How does this affect your other loyalties?"

"What 'other loyalties'?" There were a handful of Company employees I suspected were also in The Order. Case wasn't one of them.

"You didn't move around growing up like I did. You have friends here that go back a long time, right?"

"Oh...that. Colvin, I've got The Job, I've got Caroline. Nothing else really matters that much."

* * *

"Did you think you were the only one?"

What was left of my Sauroid assault team had reacted to the shot the same way I had were lined up against the corridor wall with weapons pointed back where the shot came from. Behind me, what was left of a supposedly immortal archangel was beginning to leak what looked an awful lot to me like human blood. A few yards further down, the vault-like door to a containment chamber remained shut.

At the other end of the corridor, my boss was still pointing a .45 Magnum in my general direction. He'd traded his suit coat for a ballistic vest and covered his thinning hair with a black field cap, was otherwise dressed the same as every time I'd ever seen him in the last five years, right down to the goddam tie, tie clip, and fucking cufflinks.

Behind him stood a triad of Greys, not drones, the tall ones that apparently do the thinking. Popular fiction almost gets it right: They are essentially humanoid insects from a very different universe. Behind them, a rifle squad of sasquatches had taken aim at my team. I hadn't quite realized I was doing it, but by the time I actually saw Case, my own sidearm was pointed back at him.

What used to be called a "Mexican standoff," except I'd not been in one in ten years of Central American field work. The term was no longer considered politically correct and probably not applicable to interdimensional space aliens.

Case turning up was pretty close to the last thing I expected. Whatever had been done to him was either very recent or very subtle. Maybe both. I had never suspected a thing. "The only one what, Case? By the way, sorry about the status reports. I've been a little busy."

"Your lead analyst has filled in admirably. We should consider promoting him."

"Sure. Which organization did you have in mind?"

Case chuckled. "The only one that matters. The one you could've been part of if a pack of drug-addled hippies hadn't gotten to you first. The one you can still join unless you plan on continuing to stand between me and what I came here for."

"The Archangel Array? You could've had it any time you wanted it between splashdown and winding up here. You want it now? There's nothing keeping you from going around me."

"Not the array. Not even the object that struck it down. The thing directly behind you."

"There nothing 'directly behind me' except a buddy of mine you just shot dead in the back, you son of a bitch. Ask nice, and maybe I'll think about it."

This time Case laughed out loud. "He's no more dead than you're in a position to bargain. I don't think he can die, but as long as that bullet's in him, whatever promises he made you are null and void."

"What is it, a silver bullet? You want him, you come and take him... you just gotta get through me."

I took the safety off my sidearm with a loud and deliberate click. "You're a desk jockey, Case, and I was taking out bigger men than you while you were still figuring out what your dick was for. You think you're up for it? Bring it."

"Not silver, not really a bullet or anything else you've ever heard of, and not important, it'll work as well as lead where you're concerned, and I have five more. But you're still a valuable asset, and you've been a friend, even if you're a posturing old punk rock cowboy asshole. You have one more chance to stand down."

I shook my head. "Sorry, you want him? You gotta come get him."

"Actually," Case said. "I don't." Switching to a one-handed grip on the revolver, he made a gesture that seemed awfully familiar. I felt a tingling sensation around my face and my head.

Suddenly, the rolled-up balaclava was stripped away.

Then he stripped away the tinfoil hat.

Then he stripped away me.

* * *

Finally, it had become inevitable.

The fights became more frequent, the makeup sex after the fights went away. The occasional drinking turned into constant drinking. The occasional bitter, drunken accusations turned into constant bitter, drunken accusations.

It became obvious that I'd left behind everything else I knew and loved for someone who no longer loved me, no longer wanted me, and needed 'space' that I had never needed, wanted, or even understood.

I'd put everything I had into one desperate effort at trying to make her happy…and failed. Even if she'd offered me a second chance, I couldn't take it. I'd made bargains I couldn't break and painted myself into a corner. Worse yet, I had finally gotten old.

It was supposed to be a long overdue trip to places in the world she wanted to see, including a few where my past could easily have caught up with me in ways I couldn't even begin to explain. Neither one of us called it a "separation." "Divorce" was a word I couldn't even say to myself.

But we knew.

Neither one of us said a word on the drive to the airport. I'd put the top down despite the drizzle. I stole glimpses of her when I could take my eyes off the road, trying to embed as much of her in my mind and memory as I could. She either stared ahead or look down at her phone. She would not look at me.

As always, I run the tape back in my mind and try to figure out what else I could've said, what else I could've done. As always, the tape in my mind still winds up with me at an airport, watching my entire world walk away with an overloaded backpack, never to return.

We stood at the long corridor to the security gate. I couldn't really hug her because of the backpack, but I kissed her until she made me stop. "I'm going to come back," she whispered, but I knew it wasn't true.

Then she turned and walked away. I watched, incapable of moving.

Then she was at the gate.

Then she turned.

Shrugging off the backpack, she walked back. Never in her life had she been more beautiful.

I could not move, only watch as she walked toward me, smiling, radiant.

Finally, she was standing before me. "I was wrong, Murphy. Wrong about everything. We can try again. Will you give it all up? Give it up for me?"

"I'm sorry, baby," I whispered. "I can't."

The smile on her face turned to horror as I raised the gun.

I pulled the trigger.

* * *

"Nonlethal settings," was what I had told the team.

Case glared up at me, paralyzed, from where I'd dropped him a yard away. In my hand was the Sauroid sidearm I'd just fired. It was tricked up to look like a Glock 9mm, with an extra control surface accessible to either a human or sauroid thumb. I gestured with it at the end of the corridor.

"Light 'em up!" I screamed at my team, dropping to the floor and dropping the fake Glock.

Case's Magnum was an easy reach away. I ripped it from his hand. The Grey triad had not moved from the end of the corridor.

Three shots later, I retrieved my tinfoil hat and balaclava, better safe than sorry. The Magnum got tucked into my jacket.

Returning to my feet and holstering the fake Glock, I turned to my second in command. "Gimme your knife," I told him.

nine: murgenstaern

Light returned to both my inner and outer vision.

Murphy was standing over me, his leather jacket spattered with large amounts of what looked like human blood.

"Are you injured?" I asked.

"Nope, this would all be yours, took a while to find the bullet." He held up a black anodized combat knife, also bloody, and turned to his Sauroid second in command. "Nice knife," he said, flipping it in the air and catching it by the blade point. "If I'd used the backup sticker in my boot,

129

I'd still be digging. Thanks for the loan." He extended the blade hilt first to the Sauroid, who returned it to a belt scabbard without comment.

It was difficult, but I could stand. Murphy helped me. The damage to my 'puppet' was not trivial. Luckily, I would not need it much longer.

"I... I don't know how to describe this." I said. "My senses went away. What happened?"

"You got shot, old son, in the back, by this piece of shit." Murphy kicked another human, lying bound at his feet. "Lucifer Morningstar, meet Colvin Case, one way or another, my now ex-boss."

"That makes no sense. How could a bullet make me insensate?"

"Oh, this is a very special bullet," Murphy said, retrieving an object from his pocket and holding it up: a small and strangely opaque spheroid. "It contains a miniature version of the same machinery that paralyzed you on the trip down here... except this up close and personal, it completely knocked you out."

"If by 'knocked out,' you mean 'unconscious,' not so. But all of my senses... stopped. I have never experienced such a thing, not in all of time."

"Trust me," Murphy said. "You get used to it."

* * *

It was a strange experience, having someone explain to me events of which I had no knowledge.

Stranger still: To find out how many events had occurred without my knowing... for far longer than I had ever known.

The Greys had engineered the entire thing. They had found the Seraphim Stone in the depths of space, caused it to arrive on Earth... all for the sole purpose of again attempting to abduct me.

"What else happened?" I asked Murphy.

"Not much. Just a firefight, a few Greys getting shot, and me getting assfucked in the mind by the same piece of shit that shot you." He kicked the other human again. "Nice trick, Case. Greys teach you that?"

"Teaching isn't exactly what they do, Murphy." The monkey named 'Case' was restrained with zip ties at his ankles and wrists. Another zip tie had been used to secure one of the Faraday cage skullcaps to his head. Between bruises and damage to his clothing, it seemed likely he'd been kicked a few times while I was unaware. "I received benefits in return for favors," Case said. "No different than you and The Order."

"Oh, it's a lot different," Murphy said. "How long have you known?"

"That you were an agent of The Order? Not long, really."

"How about you? When did the Greys turn you?"

"That's not what they do, either. They never had to 'turn me'. They made me."

"A hybrid?" Murphy's expression was somewhere between incredulity and disgust. The incredulity, at least, I understood. Sauroids have more common DNA with humans. So does a terrestrial insect, for that matter.

"If you want to call it that," Case said. "I never believed any of this was real. I thought I'd just had recurring nightmares as a kid. A year ago, the nightmares came back." He laughed. "I still don't think it's real, but here I am." He looked up at Murphy. "So now what?"

Murphy squatted next to his prisoner and removed a handgun from his jacket, different from the sidearm he'd had earlier. "What you did to me when you were trying to get through me to Morningstar was about the shittiest thing I've ever gone through outside a Colombian jail. I don't know how much of that was intentional and how much of it was just a suggestion, and I don't want to know."

He placed the barrel tip beneath Case's jaw and pushed up. "There's two rounds left in this thing, and I've had a shitty day. As for 'now what,' that has a lot to do with your buddies up there."

"They've gone," Case said.

Murphy turned to me. "Can you confirm that?"

I nodded. "My senses are as they were. The mothership has departed."

"How about you? If you were really human, you'd either be on a gurney or a slab right about now."

"My puppet has sustained worse damage than this and soon will not matter. I think that it is finally time that I was on my way."

"I reckon so," said Murphy.

ten: murphy

I've been in worse fights. Giving guns to sasquatches is just a bad idea in general. The big guys are pacifists by nature. But they do what the Greys tell them to do, which is one of the reasons I'd used Case's Dirty Harry hogleg to put a headshot each in the triad running the operation.

I'd also hoped taking them out might mean the mothership leaving. They're a hive organism, after all, despite being more or less humanoid. If the triad that showed up to snag Morningstar and the Stone was also in command of the mothership, there was a good chance the hive on the ship would return to base, either by instinct or command.

Also, shooting Greys gave me something else to do besides shoot Case... which was still pretty damned far from out of the question.

I'd had no particular reason to believe Case when he told me that Morningstar wasn't dead, but also no reason not to. It didn't take much field surgery with a borrowed knife to realize that what he called his 'puppet' was just that: A meat puppet with the necessary organs to imitate a man and nothing more, which also made it easier to retrieve the bullet. It wasn't exactly bloodless surgery, but nothing compared to what would've happened if I had dug a hole that size in a human.

The assault team had shot about half a dozen sasquatches before the rest of them surrendered. None of the sasquatches were dead or injured; the Sauroid weapons had all been set on stun.

"I thought I told you guys to just use 'non-lethal' for humans," I'd said to my second in command.

"All you monkeyss look the ssame to usss," he replied. "We can ssstil kill them if you like."

"Naw, that's fine."

The convulsion that had happened when the bullet came away confirmed that Case had at least told part of the truth. As I was applying a field dressing, Morningstar's eyes opened, and he asked if I was injured. I explained that the blood was all his.

Questioning Case raised more questions than answers. I'd had him restrained as soon as the firefight ended, still wanted to kill him. The hallucinations he'd caused me to have left me feeling like there was a hole in my heart the size of the one I'd dug in Morningstar... or maybe just reopened the hole that was already there.

Finally, it was obvious. It was time to finish what we'd come here to do.

"Are you still our ticket out of here?" I asked Morningstar.

He nodded. "The closer I get, the more I can feel it. Once I have the Seraphim Stone, I can transport you all. What do you propose to do with Case and yonder corpses?"

"Leave 'em," I said. "This place has a big freezer, and I'm sure they'd love to add more Greys to their collection. Whether they add Case to the collection or not is up to them."

I'd helped Morningstar to his feet, but he didn't need any help after that. He still looked like he should be horizontal, room temperature, and waiting for a toe tag. But appearances in his case, excuse a vast understatement, were frequently deceiving.

I gave orders to the Sauroids, left them guarding the sasquatches, and assured them we would all soon be out of here. Then, I followed Morningstar to the door to the containment chamber.

He entered 'statue mode' for so long I wondered if he'd lied about the extent of his damage. Then the door opened, sliding away on massive steel tracks.

And then we were in. We walked past a row of hazmat suits, and I wondered briefly if I needed one. But only briefly. I decided I would trust Morningstar. I would at least live long enough to see an end to this, no matter what.

Then an inner airlock door which yielded even more easily to the force of an archangel's mind, and then the containment chamber itself.

It was huge, the size of a stadium. The burned and broken remnants of the Archangel Array had been arranged into roughly its original shape, a brick-shaped object maybe a hundred yards long, twenty to thirty across. By following the fragmentation lines, it was easy enough to see where the impact had occurred.

As we approached the wreckage, Morningstar halted. "Best you not proceed," he said.

"Is it safe to even be in here?"

"It is, at a distance." He turned to me and extended a hand. He still looked like either a eurotrash banker or an aging gigolo. It was easy enough to take him for human unless you've had the kind of trade craft training that assumes absolutely nothing...or if you had seen him in action.

"I do not know if I will be able to do this once I have taken up the Seraphim Stone, so I should like to do so now: Offer my hand one last time after the manner of your kind. I have had allies and adversaries on this world...even a few friends, at least some of which have known me for at least some of what I am. But you have the distinction of being the last and perhaps truest of my friends here, for you are the friend who is helping me to go home."

I took the hand that I knew could easily crush my own, more like marble to the touch than ever. "Thank you, Morningstar. You may not realize it, but you've helped me as well, old son. And I'm glad you get to go home."

Then he walked on through the satellite wreckage toward the thing that looked like a rock. As he drew closer, the rock, the Seraphim Stone, began to glow, and so did he. The golden hair became like fire. His clothing smoldered and fell away from a body that was now as bright as burnished brass and then like molten gold.

Brighter, brighter still…then too bright to look upon. I held my arm before my face and thought of stories of mortals burned to ash by seeing gods too closely. Then, when I thought the light could grow no brighter, it was suddenly everywhere. And then just as suddenly gone.

* * *

It took me a moment to realize that where I was wasn't where I'd been the moment before. It took me another moment to realize it was a place I knew.

"Is this sufficient for a 'ride'?" The voice came from behind me, where there was suddenly light as well. It was a familiar voice but altered. I turned.

"Is this your 'true form'?" I asked.

"No," said Morningstar. "You could not perceive my true form. Still just a disguise, but it seemed appropriate. Indulge me."

Lucifer Morningstar stood twenty feet tall, with hair like a crown of flame and skin like glowing marble. He was naked, and if his disguise had ever included genitalia, he'd decided he no longer needed it. He was sexless as a Ken doll or G.I. Joe but muscled more like He-Man. Gone as well was my earlier 'field surgery.'

"The wings are a nice touch," I said. "Do they work?"

"Merely symbolic, but the meaning should be evident."

"It is." We were in Morningstar's lair under the mountain, close enough to my own home that I could walk there, or to the Lyin' Lamb, which didn't seem like a bad idea. The opening in the roof I'd once dropped a car through was open, stars showing through it. "I recall promising a few other people rides as well," I said.

"The promises we both made have been kept," Morningstar replied. "The sasquatches are among their own kind, and the sauroids are back on the mountain where we first found them. Case and his dead employers were left behind, as you asked."

"Then that's it," I said. "The cosmos awaits, old son, and I recall you also promised some folks you'd soon be on your way."

"Indeed I did, and indeed I shall, even though I recall no timetable mentioned, and the 'folks' to whom you refer take almost as long a view of things as I do. I have one last bit of business I need to attend to... and then I shall go.

"That business is you, Murphy. I promised things to you that you shall have. But you deserve more. I am not so great as I once was, but restored to more than I have been in many millions of years. Before I go, I will settle this debt. Anything you want on this world is mine to grant. You have but to ask."

"Really?" I laughed. "You're granting me a wish?"

"If you like."

"What I want, not even you can give me unless you can turn back time or make Caroline love me again. Can you?"

"The first is beyond my abilities, the second beyond my understanding... and not something I would do, regardless. Name something else."

Yeah, there was something else. Something I suddenly knew I had to do.

"I don't know if you know what Case did while you were out of it, I don't know if it's even anything I could explain or if it was even intentional, but it was the cruelest damned thing I've ever had done to me. I know why all those other poor bastards on the base were either curled up and catatonic or dead. Only an adept of The Order would even begin to be able to fight back against something like that, and I almost didn't... and it left me wounded like I've only been wounded once before."

"I am sorry for what you endured."

"Yeah, me too." It was a bad idea, but not much worse than any others I'd had lately. "I just want to see her again, Morningstar. I just want to know she's okay. I just want to tell her again that I love her. I want to see Caroline."

"It is unwise, but I know that you know that. And that you do not care."

"Right on both counts."

"Very well, my friend." He turned statue for a moment, then pointed to a corner of the room. "Done."

Caroline looked a little different from the last time I'd seen her, except for her clothes. She was wearing an oversized t-shirt and not much else. Her hair was longer and messy. I had no idea what time it was, but apparently, she'd been in bed. She may or may not have had a clue that she was beautiful.

But I knew.

She looked at her hands for a long moment, then said, "weird...I don't think I'm dreaming." She looked up and saw me. She closed her eyes for a long moment, looked again, and apparently decided I was real. I started to walk toward her.

She backed away. "Whatever the hell is going on, Murphy, it is way not cool. There are laws against this sort of thing, not that you ever gave a shit about the law." She then looked past me at Morningstar. "Oh, fuck. What the hell is that?"

I sighed. "That is a long story, and time's short. Let's just say he's a friend, and I've been doing some off-the-books consulting again. He owes me a favor, offered me anything in the world I wanted, but all in the world I really wanted was to see you again."

"Yeah." She snorted derisively. "That's nice. Does your friend have a name?"

"Many," said the angel. "But the one I like best is 'Morningstar.'"

"I'm going to pretend all this is real for as long as it takes to wind up back in bed with my fiance and be able to tell myself it didn't really happen.

"I can't think of one single thing we didn't talk to death before I left, Murphy. If you've something important enough to say that I need to be standing in a cave in my jammies hanging out with my ex and, oh, fuck me. A twenty-foot-tall naked angel? How can this be anything?"

"It's a big world, baby," I said, "and there's a lot you don't know, a lot you can't know, for your own damned good."

"Including a lot about you, but I knew that already. OK, I thought I knew that."

"The stories were all true, Caroline. The drug running, the questions about who I really worked for, all of it. There was more, as well, but we don't have time for all that. I'm sorry I kept secrets from you. I wanted to tell you everything, but I couldn't."

"I guess not."

"One of the things I couldn't tell you was how many favors I had to pull in so we could move and I could keep my job. I really thought you'd be happy, and I put everything I had into making it work, not just the money from my mom and dad... *everything*.

139

"By the time I knew it wasn't going to work, I didn't have any options. It wasn't that I didn't want to do the things you wanted. I couldn't. And I couldn't even tell you why.

"It wasn't even just that. When we left Houston, you mostly just wanted to get out. I wanted to find a home. You still wanted to see the world. I'd already seen more of it than I wanted. I didn't really realize it until you left, but I'd gotten old, and you were still young. It wasn't fair for you to be stuck with me."

"No...it wasn't."

"I get that now, and I'm sorry I didn't get it before. But I could never have left you, baby. I'd have sooner died."

"I know, Murphy. That's why I had to go."

Looking at her hurt, but so did not looking at her. "The home I meant for us is my home now, and it's not too bad. Getting old isn't so bad, either. I will always, always love you, and this way, the thing that worried me most will never happen."

"What thing was that?" she asked.

"I didn't want you to see me die. Even after I took the desk job, I always worried that some old business might catch up with me. Then, after it looked like I'd dodged that one, I realized I didn't want you to see me die of old age, either."

"Murphy, I love you too. But I'm glad I'm not with you anymore. The things I didn't know about you were driving me crazy, but I can't imagine how I could've lived with... any of this."

"Yeah, me neither."

"I want you to promise me something, though," she said. "And then please send me home."

"Sure, anything."

"Just because you feel old doesn't mean you are old. Your parents lived a long time, so will you.

"Don't be alone, Murphy. Find someone you can share this with, all of it, no more lies. That's what I want you to promise me."

I walked toward her again. This time, she didn't back away. "Is it OK if I kiss you goodbye?"

"Sure, no tongue, though, and keep your hands to yourself, mister."

Under Morningstar's impassive gaze, I held my wife for what I knew would be the last time. After a moment, her arms were around me as well.

Then I did kiss her.

After a time, I broke the embrace with one arm still around her. I muttered a phrase in a very old language and passed my hand before her eyes. "Sleep," I said and lowered her into the nearer of the two overstuffed chairs.

Stepping away, I looked away. "Send her home," I whispered.

"Done," said Morningstar. I looked back, and of course, she was gone already.

"Time I were bound for home as well, though not quite so quickly or easily," Morningstar then said. "One promise alone remains before my promise to quit this place quickly." He raised one enormous fist and gazed at it, turning statue for a moment. Then he opened his hand. "Take this," he said, tossing me what he'd held.

I snagged it from the air. It was a thumb drive, no different from half a dozen in a desk drawer in my office. High-end, but definitely a stock item.

"Everything you need to know about the things I leave behind on Earth is there. I suggest you make copies. The doors to this place will open to your touch. Dawn will break soon, and you can go home."

"Thank you. I guess this is it, then."

"It is." He looked up at the sky, then looked back to me. "Very few among your kind or any other have known me for any real part of what I truly am and still been a friend or ally. You have been both. I shall actually miss you, Murphy."

"No, you won't."

He smiled. It was the first time I had ever seen him do so when he wasn't pretending to be human. "You would be surprised. Farewell, my friend."

He spread the purely symbolic wings and gazed upward again. The burnished silver of his body grew bright from within, soon too bright to look upon. Then the light was gone.

I looked up. Even though my eyes were dazzled, I could still see a bright spark in the sky ascending to heaven.

Epilogue

one: murphy

Not surprisingly, archangels with superhuman senses don't need nightlights. Or lights at all, really. By starlight, I found the chair I'd put Caroline in, collapsed into it myself, and slept for a long, long time.

The gray light of a typical Pacific Northwest day eventually awakened me. I figured out where the door was and how to use it. Not surprisingly, it was raining. I flipped up my jacket collar and pulled my cap down to my eyebrows, then trudged down the trail to the park.

When I got to my condo, the old Porsche I had left in the hold of a flying saucer was parked in front of my garage with a wax-sealed parchment envelope under one wiper blade.

Breaking the seal, I found a single large feather from the wing of an owl and a folded scrap of notepaper. The note simply said "call me" in Evangeia de Lourdes' archaically precise penmanship.

Eventually, I did.

It turned out that Colvin Case had been a better friend than I'd thought. The telecommute program that had enabled me to move to the Northwest had been his idea all along. Even though I wasn't the only person who'd benefited from it, it was obvious from the policy inception date it had been rolled out for me.

His successor did not consider the policy a success or consider me a particularly valuable asset. I was offered a decent pension package and an early retirement. I took them. Apparently, the fact that I had led a team of humanoid lizard commandos into the guts of a secured facility under attack by Flying Saucers and Bigfoot was going to remain my little secret. One among many.

The earnest young technician who showed up to collect my modem and my Company laptop was remarkably non-committal on the non-booby-trapped condition of the modem, so much so that he was almost certainly another mole for The Order. But neither he nor I offered up any secret handshakes. I was just glad to get the shit out of my house.

It had been enlightening to make a return visit to Morningstar's lair under a neighboring midget mountain when I had time to explore it in the daylight. I found an extensive collection of men's suits a bit too big for me to wear and apparently dating back over a century, judging from the items that had not yet rotted away to dust.

I also found a large collection of flat-screen TVs and other consumer electronics, all powered by a discretely positioned solar panel array. There was also a large bin full of paper and metal currency, some of it as old as some of the disintegrating suits. The most valuable thing on the premises was an impressively well-stocked wine cellar.

If this was typical of his other lairs, what Morningstar had given me was of mostly antiquarian value. I had neither time nor resources to explore them all. I offered them up to The Order for a price that nicely supplemented my pension from The Company. Not all of them. The copy of the data I eventually handed over to Evangeia had a few strategic deletions, but it was complete enough to pass inspection.

No one really retires from The Order, but it was understood that my usefulness as a strategic resource was pretty much at an end. Recent events notwithstanding, I had never been seen as a tactical resource, and I was happy to keep it that way. As long as I continue to keep the secrets I promised to keep, I am free to live out my life as I see fit.

When one of the houses on the winding road that traverses Morningstar's mountain went on the market, I picked it up and sold the condo that had been mine and Caroline's home. It's a smaller place, but these days, it's just me and the cats. Not to mention, there's one helluva view from my new deck.

Also, no memories.

I added a wine cellar and a couple of other improvements. My contractor thought the cellar was entirely too deep. "Never know what you'll find around here," he told me. "There are caves all through this mountain. Indians dug tunnels as well, so did bootleggers. Some folks even think Bigfoots use the caves. I don't believe that."

"I don't either," I told him. "But I do believe I'm paying you enough to do as I ask without a lot of questions."

"You are that," he said.

I'm not really retired. There will probably always be a need for people with my particular skills and institutional knowledge... but being a freelance consultant has a lot of advantages.

I still drink at the Lyin' Lamb; have even managed to convince some of the other techies and recruiters who hang out there to hook me up with the occasional gig. Age discrimination is perhaps less a thing than I thought it was. Or maybe it helps that I'm strictly freelance and strictly a consultant.

I have still not kept my last promise to Caroline, but that's not going to be an easy one. I don't really want to be anyone else's disappointment, and being alone isn't quite the same thing as being lonely. And finding someone who could share my life, all of it, is one serious tall order.

What little I've heard from Caroline since the last time I saw her pretty much confirms that she decided to take that last time as a dream after all... and who can blame her? Even if it weren't for people like me making sure the latest sasquatch, reptilian, or UFO sighting got written off as the current version of swamp gas, most people would edit these things out of their consciousness, anyway. There are more things in heaven or earth than dreamed of in most of our philosophies, and the vast majority of us like it that way just fine.

As for Morningstar, it seems that he was as good as his word: He is well and truly gone. How quickly he can return to the center of all things, whether or not he will reunite with his Creator before Time's end...these are questions above my paygrade, perhaps beyond any mortal speculation. Surely, he is more happy; surely, he deserves it.

I still don't know how much to believe of him. Between the evidence of my senses and the guidance of Occam's Razor, taking him at his word makes more sense than not. It probably helps that I've known and had to deal with other basically immortal beings.

As for me, the pain and loss of my own short mortal life seems easier to bear now. If an immortal from the beginning of time can keep faith with a promise for most of eternity, keep that promise, and find their way home, who am I to say what is or is not possible? Who am I to say the love I still have for the person I can't help but still think of as 'my wife,' a love I'll likely have until the end of me, if not the end of time, is futile or somehow in vain? Oh, I've 'moved on' in all the ways that matter will never again trouble or complicate her life. But she's a complication in mine as long as I have one...and I wouldn't have it any other way.

There is an old saying within The Order that a true initiation never ends. Transmuting my own pain and helping Morningstar find a way past his has taken me further into the deeper reality of my own onetime initiation than has anything else. It's sufficient for now... but I would be a fool to suppose that it ends here.

But stories end, even if initiations don't, and this is as good a place as any to end this one...at least for me.

two: morningstar

The stars, blue shifted, flare into view before me. Red shifted, they fade in my wake.

I both lied and did not lie to Murphy when I told him I would miss him. It saddens me that the insouciant old monkey is almost certainly now dust, But mine are the senses and memories of an angel. Every microsecond of the time spent with him is mine to recall to subatomic levels of detail, no less so than any other moment since that moment I was called into existence... to carry forth the word and will of God.

I hope that he eventually found some measure of happiness among his own kind, but I have my doubts. Having been made aware of a greater reality is no easy thing to roll back... even at the cost of what might be considered happiness.

I will never know, of course, for I have found my way back to my own greater reality. I am not yet home, but I am on my way. How far I have gone, how far remains or how long the journey, I cannot truly say. For my sense of time is, once again, also that of an angel... measured by the progression of galaxies, not planets.

But my gratitude and love abides, both for the small, frail things I dwelt among for so long and the Creator who, for whatever unknowable reason, decided that to be my fate.

It remains an interesting question how much of this was truly fated. The universe is an unfolding fractal, a puzzle box from the mind of God. Whether free will is an illusion or not is beyond even my knowing. Count it among the questions I hope to have answered once I am well and truly returned home.

And so I proceed onward.

The galaxies, blue shifted, flare into view before me. Red shifted, they fade in my wake...

About the Author

A.J. Curry is a writer with interests including history, fantasy, science fiction, and the occult-in no particular order, and not excluding other interests as well. Their preferred beverage is a dirty martini with pepper-infused vodka.

About the Publisher

Rose City Digital is a Portland-based boutique digital agency offering a wide range of creative and technical consulting services. RCD Press is their publishing consultancy, providing services and assistance to Pacific Northwest self-published authors.

For more information, visit https://rosecity.digital.

Morningstar

© 2017, 2025 A.J. Curry

Cover

© 2017 Michael Lerch Fine Art

Published 2025 by

RCD Press, Portland, OR

979-8-9985988-2-1

Paperback

www.ingramcontent.com/pod-product-compliance
Lightning Source LLC
Chambersburg PA
CBHW071303130626
46556CB00003B/1450